DCS BOOKS PRESENTS

SAIGON

DCS Books and Publication, LLC

DAVID C STEWART

Table of Contents

Chapter One

I'm sick of this shit!" he shouted, ignorant to the few passersby casting sidelong looks in his direction. He kneeled to a tattered Nike and eyed his reflection in a store's window. He swore at his embrown skin and tired, walnut eyes. His nose was small, except for the bridge's width revealing it's been broken often in the past. Huge dimples sat in both cheeks, and a full set of cigarette-stained beauties intruded when he passed his thick, brown lips to smile.

Daewoo had freebased cocaine most of the weekend and was shocked he'd not passed out from exhaustion. He continued home, surviving on fumes, wishing for one more Vic to subdue the cruel yearning aching his chilled bones. He pulled, from his pants pocket, what remained of the quarter ounce of slum cocaine. Three dime-bags were left. He made a mental note to re-up on Bolivian Flame.

As he neared the 13th Street project, an untamed hunger tore at his gut with loud churns. He dreaded turning in hungry and knowing there was no food in the apartment. During past cocaine binges, he'd guzzle a half-gallon of water before rushing to sleep to avoid the pangs of starvation.

Fortunately, through sheer exhaustion, he'd been rewarded the comfort of obliviousness. He heard footsteps trailing him and spun. "Tone, what's up, player?" he greeted. He stopped to give the teenage addict time to catch up.

"Same shit, different day," the youngster replied. He looked past Daewoo toward the skyscrapers. "Who got somethin'?"

Tone was 19 years old, eight years younger than Daewoo, who felt awkward being quizzed about drugs by someone so young but has never faltered to reap the benefits such an opportunity presented.

"You tried Candy's? She's probably the only person up this time a mornin'."

"I ain't get there yet. You had some already?"

"Earlier. You know she got the fattest sacks down here, right?" Daewoo sized the young buck up for a switch.

Tone could easily be read as Asian. His icy, brown eyes were slanted and revealed family traits extending as far as the Orient. His 5'6" frame and light complexion furthered that notion, and often, he felt the need to explain his roots. The source was his grandfather, who'd migrated from China shortly before World War 2. Tone's father had inherited his father's eyes, and Tone suspected when he fathered a child, it, too, will carry the distinctive trait.

"Look, I'm 'bout to go in the buildin' if you need me to cop," Daewoo stated, aware of the five-dollar fee for copping someone else's high for them.

"I might need you," Tone replied. "But dig, I'm a look out for you with one."

"Bet! That's what's up!"

"You think I'm a be able to get in?" Tone asked. "You know the guards be trippin'."

"Don't even worry 'bout that," Daewoo coaxed. "Old man Dokes should still be workin'. Shit, he might be sleep-- or got some young piece somewhere trickin'."

"Yeah? He be trickin' like that?" Tone trilled as the two started toward Saigon.

Saigon was massive. An eleven-story redbrick with four rows of squared windows running its length. At the building's entrance, Daewoo turned to Tone. "Wait here. I'm a see what's up. I might can get you in if I say you my cousin."

Tone waited while Daewoo entered the building and remembered why visitors and residents nicknamed the high-rise Saigon.

The stench of urine and garbage singed his nose as the huge metal doors banged shut behind him. "Where he at?" Daewoo mused, peeking in the bulletproofed booth used to supervise the lobby.

For eight years, security's been provided for residents of Martin Luther King Projects. Saigon's reputation alone convinced city officials that security was needed, not only there, but throughout housing projects across Pennsylvania.

However, only a small fraction of residents felt protected with security monitoring the area on foot, as well as who visited the buildings. Unfortunately, for the complacent, many housing officers fell prey to the environment. In one of the four eleven-story buildings, a headquarters had been constructed in hopes of deterring the determined few who deemed it necessary to: deal drugs, rob, and steal. Overall, the security was welcome. Many were even invited to barbecues, card parties, and other social gatherings—still, in every crop lurks its rotten few, who entertain as well in hopes of imposing their lawless-ness. In many cases, they proffer sex, but mostly they offer the root of all evil. Money.

Today, Daewoo figured, old man Dokes was in the bathroom trickin'. He backtracked to the entrance and beckoned Tone to hurry. Maybe today wouldn't be ruined as he imagined, Daewoo thought. Instead of the cocaine Tone had promised, he'd ask for cash and get a meal.

At the elevator, Tone turned to Daewoo. "You think she'll give up five for twenty?" he asked.

"I don't think so. She tight as hell 'bout that money."

"Yeah, I know. I can't stand that stuck up bitch!" Tone spat.

"Oh, you copped here before?"

"A few times. She be frontin' like I'm 5-0 or somethin'." Daewoo snickered, wondering how anyone could mistake Tone for a cop. He believed Tone must have spooked her. A few years back, Daewoo had heard about two shootings Tone had supposedly been involved in. One, Daewoo was certain of. In fact, now that he's mulled over how wild Tone was, he squashed the idea of trying to switch bags of coke on him and chose to settle on the measly five spot.

Daewoo watched as the elevator door crept half-open. Its three florescent bulbs hanging on their last legs and blinking instantaneously. Urine covered the riveted metal floor, and collages of graffiti lined the walls giving an encore to the diseased tank.

While Daewoo pushed 8 on the console, Tone fished out two five-dollar bills and a ten. He handed Daewoo a five then thought how he hated spending his last few dollars with Candy. He hated the attitude she gave him. The cold stares and turned up nose drove him mad. It was her "I'm better than you" attitude that pissed him off. He reminisced about *his* days on top. When *he* sold coke. For Tone, those days were wonderful.

Tone was sixteen when he first entered the drug game and buck wild. Although he was younger than most dealers, he received equal status, if not more. He used to love how the bootlicking junkies flocked around him, anticipating crumbs for obeying his commands. Everyone craved his friendship then, and his youthful vulnerability made him eager to share his good fortune. Now that he'd fallen to the exact thing, which had placed him on a pedestal, he could count each mistake beginning with his first snort of cocaine. Back then, if anyone would've implied his snorting would lead to freebasing, he'd have torn them a new asshole. Yet, here he stood, on a pissy elevator early in the morning, trying to cop. What a change, he thought. To be on the outside looking in must seem funny.

By the time the elevator reached the eighth floor, Tone had convinced himself that everyone now thought of him as a joke.

He recalled a pledge he'd made to himself during his dealing days. Never take shorts and never tolerate disrespect.

Besides the humming of the elevator's descent, the narrow hallway was quiet. Candy's apartment was next to the staircase at the hallway's end.

Tone listened at the door for movement inside. He knew, from previous buys, that Candy and her husband lived alone. "Hold up, Daewoo. Wait on the steps. You know she don't like serving two people."

"Man, she knows who I am," Daewoo protested. "I live right down the hall."

"Just wait on the steps," Tone persisted, fixing Daewoo with an icy stare.

Daewoo took the hint and reluctantly entered the stairwell.

He closed the stairwell door and listened.

Tone knocked.

The reaction of slippers sliding across the apartment floor indicating Candy was open for business. He heard the locks and chains fall from the door, but at the sound of the door opening, a crash erupted, then Tone's venomous words, "MOVE BITCH! GET THE FUCK BACK!"

Daewoo couldn't believe Tone was sticking up Candy. Refusing to budge, he held his breath, listening to the small, muffled screams. To him, it sounded as if Tone was covering Candy's mouth with a hand. Seconds later, when things quieted, Daewoo eased from the staircase and stood in front of Candy's apartment in awe. He strained to hear any sounds of a struggle. He heard none. On the floor were droplets of blood and Candy's overturned, terry-cloth slipper. "Awe shit," he sighed. He trailed the red specks for twenty feet and found their source in a bedroom, perched on an unmade bed, crying and bleeding profusely from her nose. Next to Candy, her husband sat half holding the bedspread to his wife's bloody face. Daewoo saw the terror and curiosity on their faces when they saw him in the doorway. He'd no idea whether to run or help the pair. Tone helped his decision by whirling in his direction.

"Yo, what the hell you are doing?" Daewoo hollered, cringing at the sight of the huge .45 caliber.

"Just be cool. I got this shit here under control!"

"You ain't gotta do this, rodie," Daewoo pleaded.

"Nigga, please! This bitch thinks she all that 'cause she got a little coke hustle goin' on. Fuck that. She givin' that shit up." Tone grabbed Candy by her checkered robe, reached back, gun in hand, and landed a wicked blow across her face.

Blood splashed from Candy's mouth and onto the sallow wall the instant he made contact.

"Where the hell is it!" Tone screamed, brandishing the gun in the husband's face to eliminate a hero.

"Candy, give it to him, please!" the husband begged. Daewoo was blind to what Tone was capable of. He stood motionless, wondering about what he'd gotten himself into. If the rumors were true, he questioned, then what would stop Tone from shooting someone now? Not chancing he'd be the one shot, he watched nervously as Tone held the gun to the old man's head. "Look," Tone challenged, "I'ma ask your ass one more time. If you lie again, I'm a blow this old mutherfucker's head clean across this room. Where's the coke?"

"O.K…O.K.…please, don't shoot him!" Candy cried, sputtering blood from an already swollen mouth. "I'll give it to you…just don't shoot him." She reached between the mattresses and extracted two clear sandwich bags filled with money and coke. "Here! Take it and get the hell out!" she roared, throwing the bags in Tone's face.

Tone reached her in two furious strides. Again, he wacked her across the face with the gun, sending teeth spewing from her mouth. She released a howl that made Daewoo cringe.

"Come on, man," Daewoo pleaded. "You got what you wanted. Let's go."

Tone turned to him and sneered as if he was enjoying the moment. "Shut the fuck up!" he spat. "Is this it?" he screamed at the injured woman.

Candy sat conjuring a wad of saliva, blood, and broken teeth in her mouth. Her face became placid as she gathered her emotions, faced her attacker, and spit in his face. "You fucking crackhead!" she yelled, then watched delighted, Tone's shocked expression as he staggered backward.

"You stinking bitch!" Tone stormed before raising the .45 and pulling the trigger.

Candy's frail body bucked backward when the first bullet struck above her heart. Two others caught her torso mid-flight and sent her already dead body onto her husband, who's eyes bulged from their sockets.

Tone slowly approached the bed, pointed the gun to Candy's head, and watched the next bullet split her skull.

"Oh, my god!" the husband screamed while trying to push his wife's riddled body off his own.

Daewoo's heart was pounding. He stood transfixed as Tone raised the gun, yet again, this time sending a bullet through the old man's head and his tenuous frame to the bed with a soft thud.

Calmly, Tone snatched the sandwich bags from the floor and eyeballed Daewoo. "We can't have any witnesses, can we?" he commented before strolling by Daewoo and out of the room.

Daewoo stood mesmerized by the massacre. Most of his life he's lived in ghettos and this was his first time witnessing a killing. After struggling to regain his senses, he took a final look at the dead couple and left the room. The apartment's front door was still open. When Daewoo peeked into the hall to ensure no one would see him exiting the place, Tone's voice startled him.

"What the hell you peeping' for?" Tone barked. "Let's go. We got what we came for."

Daewoo, running behind Tone, took the stairs in numbers. He wrestled with Tone's use of the word *we*. What the hell he mean, *we,* Daewoo thought. We ain't got nothin' to do with this shit.

At the lobby, they both ambled to the entrance and out into the early morning air. For Daewoo, the air was refreshing. Still, as he passed by residents, he feared they'd smell the deaths on him. He knew there was no way anyone could know what had just taken place in Saigon and that his paranoia had already begun manipulating him. He'd done some awful things in the past, he thought, but nothing as severe as murder. *No way*, he thought would he take the fall for this. This was entirely too much drama.

Daewoo took a deep breath to clear his head, while Tone walking briskly in front of him, occasionally glanced back to ensure he was in tow. Daewoo realized he had to break ties with Tone as soon as possible but now wasn't the time. He clutched at each hunger pang that kicked with every breath of fresh air he inhaled. His conscience screamed for him to stop walking, to just stand still and not follow. But his hunger and cocaine craven initiated each of the steps he so desperately wanted to avoid taking. He was helpless. His greed had already enveloped him into believing the one reason he continued to follow Tone was to ensure that an understanding is made that he'd no part in the killings, despite his desire for a breakdown of the take. But first things were first, he thought, and that was to get off the streets as soon as possible.

The 8X12 cell at Graterford Prison had been constructed for one prisoner. Over the years, the populations of state penitentiaries skyrocketed, and the once single cell was doubled. Only one provision was made to accommodate a second prisoner, and that was the small iron bunkbed that dominated the tiny cell. Unlike jail cells portrayed in movies, there were no bars on the entrances, only heavy metal doors that noisily slid open and banged when they closed. A narrow metal-screened window, with two iron bars down its middle, a sink, a toilet, and a 40-watt bulb protruding from the ceiling were the only state provisions Stoney Hightower's cell contained; unless you counted the thick stench of cigarette and shit that stunk up the joint. On the bottom bunk, Stoney and his cellie indulged in a heated card game of casino while bobbing their heads to a Sade tune wailing from a small radio next to the bunk.

"Hightower! You got a chapel pass!" a burly guard yelled into the cell before keying it open.

"For what?" Stoney questioned. He turned down the radio's volume a notch.

"I don't have a clue," the guard answered before stepping off.

Puzzled, Stoney flipped the radio's volume up three notches, finished his winning hand, then grabbed his state boots. He saw no reason not to take the walk while the rest of the cellblock remained locked down for count.

The 200-yard corridor stretched the length of the jail. Every department within Graterford's wall could be reached from the passage: Activities Dept., Education Dept., Housing Areas, Barbershop, Shoe Shop, Yard, Visiting Area, Parole Offices, and even the front door hung from the corridor, mind a barred checkpoint. Even if an inmate did somehow pass the checkpoint, there was still a 50-foot cobble-stoned wall surrounding the prison. Very few escorts were necessary, and very few inmates had escaped.

The chaplain's office was located at the end of the corridor. Now, the hall had been flushed of most inmates, and prison guards stood around languidly, draped in starched grey shirts and navy-blue uniformed khakis. A few inmate workers chatted mildly with the guards while pushing long-necked push-brooms across the waxed floor. Stoney said nothing to no one as he walked. Instead, he strolled his 6'2", 230-pound frame through the hall trying to wish away the two months on a one to two-year sentence he'd received for stabbing two men during a street brawl. Stoney knew he should've seen it coming. Not many people would rumble him fairly on account of his size, strength, and skill. He even looked like a fighter. Brown-skinned, small beady eyes, a rude stare, and broad-shouldered. He possessed an aura suggesting he'd be able to handle himself in any tough situation. He glanced out of the corridor windows and thought how he'd spent most of his bit lifting weights and running ball. He'd ignored the prescriptive programs the institution had recommended he complete for parole eligibility. One stipulation was that he receive his General Education Diploma. After failing twice at that endeavor, he decided maxing out on his sentence would be easier than a third failure. Stoney was thirty-two years old and adamantly felt he'd succeed just knowing basics. When he was ten, he'd convinced his sidekicks to beg their parents and ransack their homes for pocket-change. With the change *they'd* fronted, he'd purchased paper cones, a block of ice, and several packets of Kool-Aid. Stealing sugar from home, he shaved the ice and sold flavored ice-cones to anyone with a quarter. Business had been extremely profitable for Stoney, considering his partners had only received ice-cones for their contributions. Stoney had also physically matured faster than the crew he'd romped with during childhood. This, alone, entitled him *"Policy Maker"* and, during his reign as ringleader, he'd found plenty of mischief for them all. Even today, he could still recall the cranky old women nestling on their stoops, calling him "bad ass." He'd mostly laughed and grabbed his crotch at them when they cursed his birth and shook smug heads in disbelief. Eventually, he'd outgrew his joy of shocking old women and had begun to excel in sports while slithering by academically. At fifteen, he was already six-foot, broad-shouldered, and ready for work. Instead of getting a summer job, like most kids were doing, he adopted "hustling" as a full-time gig. Eventually, the "drug-game" groomed him into what authorities considered *"penitentiary material."*

There were no signs indicating that the chapel existed just beyond two unmarked doors. One would need prior knowledge of its existence or they'd probably overlook it. Stoney knew, pushed open a door, and handed a superannuated guard his pass.

"Right there, Hightower," the guard informed him, pointing toward a large oak door in the small vestibule. Hesitant to barge in, Stoney gave the door two quick knocks before opening it. The chaplain's office was surprisingly commodious. Stoney wondered what a chaplain's job consisted of that he would need such a huge office. At the rear of the office, beneath a mural of "The Last Supper," a small, bald, Caucasian man, dressed in full clergy's uniform and spectacles, lounged behind a large, metal desk conversating on the telephone. Without pausing, he motioned Stoney to a metal chair beside the desk. Stoney sat then took notice of the place.

The office was barely furnished. It contained the marred, metal desk, two metal file-cabinets, a wooden coatrack, and one other painting portraying a mythical Jesus Crist with outstretched arms and a forgiving smile. After a few minutes, the pintsized chaplain hung up the phone and turned to Stoney. "Ah, Mr. Hightower, how are we today?" he asked, clasping his boney, freckled fingers together atop a large desk calendar, schoolboy like.

"I'm all right," Stoney replied, trying to guess the man's age.

"If you don't already know, Mr. Hightower, I'm Chaplain Becker." He paused a few seconds, as if his name would ring a bell. After noticing Stoney wasn't impressed, he continued. "Mr. Hightower, I know you're wondering why I've sent for you."

"Mmmm Hmm…," Stoney hummed. He noticed the man sucked his tongue between sentences.

"Well Mr. Hightower, I received a call today that there's been an emergency at your home."

"What kind of emergency?"

"That, I don't know. I only know that the woman, who phoned, made it noticeably clear that you need to phone this number." He slid a yellow piece of paper across the desk and spun the telephone Stoney's way. Stoney read the scrawling. He recognized his mother's phone number and his aunt's name. He dialed the number. After four rings, a female's voice answered.

"Aunt Millie?" Stoney asked.

"Who's this?"

"It's Stoney."

"Stoney?"

"Yeah, Aunt Millie. It's me. What's going on at the house?"

"Oh, Stoney, I'm so sorry, baby."

Stoney pushed the phone closer to his ear. "Sorry about what?" he asked.

"Sweetheart, you know if there's anything I can do for you, I would, right?"

"Aunt Millie, I know that. Just tell me what's wrong."
"Stoney, the police…," she summoned between sobs. "What

about the police?"

"The police…they found your mother and Paul in the house dead this morning."

"What?"

"Stoney, I'm sorry, baby."

"I don't believe this shit!" he yelled. "How?"

"They got shot," she muttered.

"Shit! Shit! Shit!" Stoney cried, slamming down the phone receiver.

The tiny chaplain leaped from his seat and eyeballed the door contemplating a quick exit. Slowly, with bated breath, he backed against the wall Stoney stared at the daunt man.

"Are you all right?" Chaplain Becker asked.

Stoney was silent. He stood shocked and disbelieving his mother was dead.

Reluctantly, the clergy stepped forward. "Mr. Hightower, if I may, I'd like to offer my deepest sympathies. Obviously, you've received some disturbing news. Is there anything I can do?"

Tears began rolling from Stoney's eyes as he recalled his last warning to his mother.

"Oh, boy, everybody knows me around here," she'd argued. "Ain't nobody fool enough to do nothin' to me knowin' your wild ass is mine."

"Mom, you can't say that" Stoney had disputed. "These crack-heads don't care nothin' 'bout me being your son. All they care about is whose they're next hit comin' from."

"Mr. Hightower. Mr. Hightower…," Stoney heard

faintly from his daze. When his head cleared, the chaplain was beside him with a sublime look.

"Would you like to share a prayer for the unfortunate?" the clergy asked.

Stoney fought against saying something foul. Instead, out of respect for his mother and stepfather, he gave the chaplain a small nod.

If not for the convictions of his own prayer, Stoney might have heard the chaplain's words. Stoney had mumbled a short prayer for his lost, then gritted another for the murderer. No way he'd let the law handle, he thought. The killers would have to pay with their lives as well.

The precinct was usually quiet on Sundays - the day when department bustle was at its minimum and the atmosphere most relaxing for the few detectives struggling to clear their desk-tops of overdue paperwork. The 2nd District's Homicide Division was located on the second floor. A near, bare flat occupying twelve metal desks opposite one another. Two-barred windows housed a sickly African Violet on its windowpane. Six of the twelve desks were occupied by detectives - among them, lodged in a window seat, sat Detective, Ryan Page pecking at an ancient Emerald typewriter. In one last fury of two finger pecks, Ryan finished up a two-day-late report, snatched it from the typewriter's jaws, and scanned it. "This ain't gonna work," he confounded, crumbling the report and jump-shooting it towards a wastebasket twenty feet away. He missed. Deciding his report would get consideration later, he sat back and evaluated his career choice. Ryan appeared much as he did in high school, minus the shadowy beard and receding hairline. His skin was a burnish cocoa. His curved lips, a rouged brown.

He ran a weathered hand through heavily jelled, jet-black hair and shucked the pencil from behind his ear onto the desk. He kicked his worn Stacey Adams up onto the desk, crossed his ankles, and concluded that life couldn't be more unpredictable. Like many negro children, Ryan had also dreamed of becoming a professional ballplayer, but his talents had fallen short of that dream becoming a reality. Instead, he'd found himself struggling through four grueling years of army life. Much of his motivation to keep fit came from his army years - and occasionally, when he'd catch himself backsliding on workouts, he'd reflect on the mental toughness it'd taken to absorb the mental barrage of egotistical drill commanders. Now, propped behind his desk, wishing he'd chosen college instead, Ryan reflected on what he might have missed out on. He pictured himself at some cushy job in some tropical paradise sipping on strawberry daiquiris. He pictured seagulls squawking behind him as the clear, blue ocean slapped against white sands. The ringing of the phone brought Ryan from his daydream. He snatched up the phone receiver and cleared his throat. "Homicide. Detective Page speaking. Mmmm. . .hmm. Mmmm…hmm. Yeah. Tell him I'm on my way."

Even at 7:25 a.m., the orb of day blazed. A tiny breeze lingered teasingly for a moment, but by the time Ryan reached the dusty, sky-blue, 1992 Plymouth Reliant, nature's tiny cough had passed. While driving recklessly toward 13th Street, he switched the air-conditioner to high and tried counting the times he's been summoned to his old neighborhood to investigate homicides. As a boy, Ryan's parents had rented a three-story home across the street from the high-rise project. He recalled bragging to other children that he didn't live in the project. He was just eleven then, but the memories lay etched in his mind.

His boasting had ceased on his twelfth birthday, when he and three pals were hoofing downtown to the Fox Theater and, unknowingly, stumbled into a rival gang's territory. When confronted and asked where they were from, Ryan's sidekicks responded, "Across Broad Street in 1241 building."

"Wrong answer," the gang's leader said before emptying their pockets one by one.

When Ryan's turn to answer arrived, he stated that he didn't live in the project but across the street. "What's the difference?" the leader chuckled before robbing Ryan as well. Afterward, the gang chased them back across Broad Street, hurling sticks, bottles, and rocks.

That day, Ryan had understood that his parents' struggles were no different than his friends' parents. Still, today, as he gunned the Plymouth through the early morning traffic, his ties to the project continued. He understood his rapport with residents were why he would be summoned, but also understood his pitfall.

Often enough, Ryan had found himself too emotionally involved in a case. His wife, Deitra, still complains about the hours he spends couped in the study and on the streets humping for leads. She'd bitched to the point where she'd finally tired, packed up the children, and decided to visit her parents for a while.

Ryan parked the Plymouth and eyeballed the crowd outside of Saigon. As he exited the car, he heard his name shouted and spun in its direction.

Captain, Roy Plummer headed his way. "Sorry about that, Ryan," he says, apologizing for startling the man.

"No problem, Captain. Just remind me to check my drawers."

"Will do," Plummer replied with a weak smile.

"So, what do we have?" Ryan asked.

"The usual crap. Nobody saw or heard a thing. I guess you know why I had them call you?"

"Why not refresh my memory?" Ryan replied haughtily.

Plummer fidgeted for the right answer. "You know," he came up with, "the way you work your magic. You do speak their language. Am I right?"

Roy Plummer was short and stubby. His face clean-shaven, eyes aqua blue with huge bags. He sported a trademark cigar between thin, pink lips. He reminded Ryan of the television detective, "Cannon."

"Well, Captain, I'm not sure if I should be flattered, but it does seem that way."

Saigon's lobby buzzed with residents, roped in a guarded area, anticipating a glimpse of the bodies being extracted. A news-crew had also arrived to fight for the best angle to shoot their account from. Ryan was disgusted at how, today, some could relish the sight of destruction. How individuals embraced such cruelties with smiles and laughter, simply because it brought attention to a place where notoriousness was admired by a generation of want-to-be's or, were they just nosey? Ryan wondered. He searched the faces for answers while Plummer grumbled an order for the elevator to be sent down.

Ryan was pleased someone had secured the elevator for evidence. Most investigators would've limited their investigation to the crime scene. Ordinarily, when crimes were committed in the ghetto, remiss investigating was condoned; although, it was the investigators' responsibility to secure evidence, witnesses, and a reasonable scenario of what had occurred. But, for decades, permissive investigating has left many inner-city residents unwilling to cooperate and most crimes unsolved. Ryan had no intention of repeating such a depressing past. Ryan and Plummer watched as the elevator door crawled open. Maintenance had replaced the flickering bulbs and cleaned the urine from the elevator's floor. The box now reeked of ammonia. They entered the elevator and scanned the punished walls for familiar names. There were a few recognizable names, but when the elevator jolt-stopped, then cruised for a while, all four eyes took notice of the escape hatch in the ceiling.

Again, the decrepit door dragged open, and both men exited exhaling held breaths. In the hallway, several uniform officers were in doorways, note-pads open, questioning occupants.

Immediately, Ryan recognized Candy Montross's apartment roped off with fat, yellow strips of tape with bold lettering that read: "POLICE CRIME SCENE." Please don't let it be her, Ryan prayed, anticipating the worst.

"Are you all right?" Plummer asked.

Ryan shrugged. "I'm not sure yet."

"Look, Ryan, I'd like for you to handle this, but, if you can't…"

"I'll be fine," he lied, already nauseous.

"We'll know in a second, won't we?" Plummer added. He took lead into the apartment. In the bedroom, two investigators busied themselves searching for prints. An enthused photographer tiptoed around the mussy bed, snapping quick, flash-bulb photos of the scene. On the floor, two zippered body-bags lay ready for transport. "Sorry to call you so late, Ryan. You know how these things get away from us," Plummer apologized.

Even as Ryan stood wretched, he knew exactly what the man meant by, "getting away from us." In other words, the homicides were back burners. He stood, absorbing the bloodied bedspreads and bullet-riddled walls.

"I got a call to make," Plummer announced before wobbling off toward the living room.

Ryan squatted at the first bag. With a shaky hand, he unzipped the bag just enough to recognize what remained of Candy Montross's face. Hurriedly, he turned his head away, zipped the bag, and viewed the next.

Paul Montross's corpse was atrocious. Nearly half of the man's forehead had been blown away - and to boot, no one had bothered closing the man's bulged eyes. Ryan did.

To Ryan, malice of this kind indicated not a botched robbery, but a vendetta had occurred. An untamed disregard for humanity that thoroughly sickened him. Not only did the display of butchery sicken him, but the idea that he could've possibly prevented the slaughter from ever happening did so as well.

He'd heard about Candy Montross dealing cocaine, but allowed their families' friendship to suffocate his oath to uphold the law. The fact that Candy had dealt small-time didn't amount to much. He concerned himself with homicides and merely turned a death ear to inner-city rituals.

He recalled the card parties his parents had hosted. The gossip, the food, the cases of alcohol consumed, and Candy Montross - always in attendance - sipping away, yacking out the goodies on those not in attendance. Ryan was supposed to have been tucked away in bed. Instead, he'd sneak to the staircase and eavesdrop on the adults dish the dirt on his friends' parents. He'd always found their prattling useful, more so when the child of the derided tried ragging on him. Ryan wondered what the palaver might consist of on a night the social had a theme such as Candy's murder. He was certain his mother would have her handful of suspects. Nowadays, she assumed anyone wearing a backward cap was a thug.

Later, after exchanging theories with other investigators, noting their findings, and securing the crime scene, Ryan searched out Captain Plummer. He found him at the living room entrance conversating with a tall, cadaverous man.

"Well, what do you think?" Plummer asked.

"I think whoever iced them didn't care much for either and had more than robbery on their mind."

"What makes you think it was a robbery?" Plummer quizzed, propping a stubbed cigar in his mouth.

"Because I knew them both," Ryan confessed. "She was dealing rock."

"Tell me about it. A scale, baggies, and a bunch of other paraphernalia were found in one of the closets. Techs bagged it," said Plummer.

"So, they knew the killer?' Sergeant Clyde Doins asked.

"I would think so," Ryan answered still fighting off seriously doubt if she'd have opened the door for just anyone. It had to be a regular, considering there's no sign of forced entry - plus, there's blood leading to the bedroom. My guess is, she opened the door for a regular and was attacked. That's the reason for their executions. "No witnesses?"

Both men nodded in agreement.

Ryan continued. "So, what I need from you, Captain, being I'm almost sure that who's ever responsible is still around, is to keep the media tamed. If I'm right, and the killers from the area, I don't want him spooked off."

"I'm sure I can pull that off," Plummer boasted. "You just keep a clear head. I don't want you getting lost on this. Got me?"

"No problem. I'll nail this asshole."

"Yeah, well, I hope so. And I hope soon. I got a meeting with the mayor about a mini station for this district. If everything goes well, I'll have to meet with residents soon. I don't need this mess hanging over my head."

Ryan let loose an exasperated breath. "Hopefully, it won't, Sir," he comforted, acknowledging how self-centered Plummer's reasons for wanting the case solved were. Ryan believed that, for Plummer, it would be just another notch on his belt on the way to some political office. Instead of dwelling on the captain's smatter of ignorance, Ryan drifted into the living room.

The living room was modishly furnished. Sofa, love chair, and recliner were all black velour with button mirrors out- lining the arm rests. Aluminum chromed, smoked glass coffee and end tables, several black ceramic carvings trimmed in gold, and a modicum of purple and black, velvet oil paintings flavored the room. Occupying a huge oak entertainment cabinet were photos, trophies, framed awards, a four-piece glass cased stereo, and a 24" television. Nothing seemed disturbed.

Ryan assumed the intruder had gotten what he'd come for. He picked up a silver-framed photo. It was taken following a City League Championship basketball game Stoney and he were rivals in. Ryan's team had dourly accepted an agonizing four-point loss. Afterward, through mostly admiration, the two be- came adversaries throughout junior high and high school. What- ever the competition had been, both attacked the vying with enormous zeal and confidence. Now that they were older, their contention has developed into a friendship of mutual respect. It used to gratify Ryan to reminisce about the past.

Unfortunately, thoughts of what Stoney's become has changed that past gratification to anguish. While he'd continued to excel academically, Stoney declined. When he heard that Stoney was in Graterford, he wasn't a bit surprised. He only hoped Stoney's stay would open his eyes. He replaced the photo and sighed at how things have turned out for his old friend.

Ryan knew that Stoney worshipped his mother. That the news would be devastating. Ryan hoped the killer would be behind bars when Stoney hit bricks. He'll certainly be hunting for revenge. And didn't take kindly to losses. In a ninth floor, abandoned apartment, across the street from Saigon, Tone and Daewoo watched curiously from a window onto the street. Neither had doubted whether the sirens they'd heard were responding to what had happened in Saigon. Still, they watched as police cars and ambulances surrounded Saigon. Daewoo paced the tenebrous tenement. "Aw, Man-!" he cried. "Why'd you shoot 'em?"

"Man, fuck that stingy ass bitch!" Tone barked. "She thought she was that, anyway, throwin' that shit in my face!"

"So what?"

"So, she shoulda just gave the coke up!"

Daewoo gave the teenager a calming frown. "Tone, you had the coke already. You didn't have'ta kill 'em. I ain't tryin'a get no bodies."

"You didn't. I did."

"Yeah, and you remember that shit too, "Daewoo replied pointedly.

"Man, stop bitchin'," Tone demanded, emptying the sandwich bags onto the floor.

The three-room tenement had been stripped of furniture appliances, doors, and all other removable features. Empty crack-vials littered the floor, and thick slabs of plywood covered the entrance and all but one dingy window.

Daewoo squatted on one of two plastic crates and eyed the floor in disgust. "This is fucked up," he whined.

"Don't worry 'bout it," Tone said. "Ain't nobody see shit."

"Yeah, well, I hope not." Daewoo produced a near-empty pack of Newport. He fished a smoke from the pack, lit it, took a deep drag, then watched Tone split the take. Halfway through the smoke, he jumped up from the crate with bulged eyes. "You know whose family that was, don't you?"

Tone looked up at the man. "No. And I don't give a fuck either."

Daewoo shook his head in rankness. "You done killed 'em and don't even know who gonna be gunnin' for your ass?"

"It don't matter."

"That was Stoney's people," Daewoo informed him.

Tone stopped counting the take, broke open the gun and checked the bullets. There were two left. "Who the fuck is Stoney?" he replied, snapping the gun back together. He returned to his task.

"Stoney that stabbed Carrot." Daewoo plucked his cigarette butt across the room.

Tone showed no concern. "Yeah, well, it's too late to worry 'bout that shit now, ain't it?"

"Not if he find out you killed his people."

Tone's head jerked up. He stared at the other addict. "And how the fuck he gonna find that out?" he asked sharply.

Daewoo regarded Tone's icy stare and became defensive. "I don't know," he shrieked. "Not from me. Hell, I'm in this shit, too, fuckin' with your crazy ass." He gave a weak smile to take the edge from his words.

Tone's stare became normal. "I told you to forget about it," Tone insisted. "You want your breakdown or not?"

"Hell yeah, I want it. You ain't bother askin' if it was cool to smoke Candy."

"Cause, I knew your ass would'a been bitchin' just like you doin' now." Tone pushed a wad of bills at him.

Daewoo stared at the money. He knew if he took the cash, there was no turning back. "Fuck it," he said, grabbing hold of the cash.

Tone held on a bit tight, causing Daewoo to snatch it. This brought a smirk to Tone's face.

As Daewoo peered down at the mob surrounding a coroner's van, he recognized a few individuals that were pointing fingers at the police. This scenario occurred whenever a tragedy erupted in the project. Residents continuously cried for more police presence in the community but would never admit that their friends and relatives were mostly responsible for the crimes.

It was always "the Whiteman," or in this case, the police, who represented the authoritative discernment.

Daewoo felt he was no better than anyone else - if not worst. He knew he was wrong, regardless of how he'd convinced himself of his innocence, and pointed his finger at Tone. By pocketing the blood-money, he'd become an accomplice to murder. Any competent D.A. would feast on him by simply establishing his presence. The words of a D.A. echoed in his mind. *"He may not have pulled the trigger, but he witnessed the killings and still.' accepted the money."* There was no jury in Pennsylvania who'd acquit him. He continued to stare at the boisterous crowd, disgusted at how easily his greed had surpassed his remorse. But as much as he wanted to leave without the cash, he couldn't. The excuses came too easily. Excuses such as: Tone would become suspicious and kill him also, second was his hunger pangs, and not to be outdone, his cocaine addiction, which gnawed at him like a pork eating preacher at a Southern barbecue. He wrestled with the idea of telling the cops but nixed the idea when he remembered the bench warrant already lodged against him. He'd keep quiet for the moment, he thought, at least if no heat was on *him* for the murders.

"Fuckin' dick head," Daewoo whispered, turning from the window.

"What's out there?" Tone asked, stuffing cocaine into a small crack-pipe.

"Just a lotta cops."

"They'll leave eventually. Just chill for a while. Here. Hit some' a this." Tone proffered the pipe.

"Nah, I don't think I can handle the skits right now."

"No. Well, I could sure use a blast after that bullshit." Daewoo squatted on the crate and watched.

The crack-pipe resembled a small bong. A small, glass sphere between two stems, one to pull from and one with a tiny bowl for feeding.

Tone illuminated the semi-dark room with a flick of his lighter to melt the coke. Tilting the bowl north, he steadied the flame beneath the crescent and, for ten seconds, inhaled the potent smoke. He pulled the pipe away and pursed his thin lips to prevent the smoke from escaping his nostrils.

Daewoo looked on aspiringly as the young gun ended his ritual by spraying a huge plume of smoke from his lungs.

The room filled quickly with the drug's enticing, sweet, sulfuric pungency.

Daewoo, tempted, squirmed on his crate as Tone placed the pipe on the floor and crept to a stand.

Each of Tone's movements was hesitant. His once small, slanted eyes were now, wide and bulged. He stood center floor, bent slightly, at the waist, with his pointer finger to his lips signaling Daewoo to be quiet. "Shhh…be quiet," he whispered, slowly twisting his head side to side. Listening.

Daewoo knew the coke must have been good. He smiled, knowing Tone must have gotten a good hit. He decided to have some fun. "Tone, sit your ass down. Ain't no-damn-body out there."

Tone spun around sharply and shushed him with an emphatic wave of his hand.

Daewoo had witnessed a variety of skitsin' once an addict received a sufficient dose of cocaine. Tone's reaction was subtle compared to others. Some addicts would disrobe, talk excessively, search clothing, tables, and floors for elusive cocaine crumbs, scratch themselves to a pulp, become horny or, encounter Daewoo's dreaded skits - paranoia. Just recently, Daewoo embraced a method to reduce his paranoia. He'd include alcohol or marijuana into his sessions. The combination of either stimulant usually curbed a phobia thar, ordinarily, carried him in and onto rooftops, alleys, old houses, beneath cars, and numerous other senseless, dangerous, and unpredictable places. Even during home sessions, he'd lock the doors, cover the door's peephole, pull the shades, and still suspect someone of watching him. His nemesis was always either the police or some smuck he conned. There were always frivolous promises to quit. Sadly, as easily as the excuses came to accept the blood money, they arose to get high again.

He decided he'd seen enough. "Tone dig this. I'm a go pick up a few 40's. What's up with you?"

"Uh-huh," Tone mumbled, breaking from his skits and tiptoeing to pick up his sweat jacket.

Daewoo had made it to the entrance before Tone caught up. "Where you goin'?" Daewoo asked.

"I'm a take the walk, too," Tone stated as he rummaged through the pockets of his blood-speckled sweatpants.

Daewoo's heart dropped. He stared disgruntled at the young fry. "I'm cool, Tone. You might as well chill 'til I get back. Plus, you all highed up."

"That little bit 'a shit I hit ain't did nothin'."

"Come on, rodie. The last thing I need is you skitsin' up and down the hall."

Tone's face broke into a sneer. "You must don't want me rollin'. You tryin'a fade?"

"Nah, it ain't like that."

"I can't tell," Tone based. "Get the hell out the way then."

Not wanting to be Tone's next victim, Daewoo stepped aside while Tone pulled the slab of wood from the hinges.

On the ninth-floor stairwell, Daewoo tried duffing Tone again. "Wait here, Tone. I don't want nobody seeing us."

The hallway's cool air had sobered Tone. He gave

Daewoo a puzzled look. "Now I know you done lost your mind. You actin' like a col' coward. If I would'a known your ass was gonna act like this, I wouldn't 'a never put your scary ass down."

"It ain't that I'm scared," Daewoo puffed.

"How the hell you ain't scared and every time I turn around, you bitchin' 'bout small shit? If you stop crying' long enough, you'll see don't nobody know shit about what happened."

Daewoo knew Tone was right and came clean. "Tone, check this out," he began dutifully, trying to find the right words without pushing the wrong buttons. "I don't even want no beer."

All I want to do is go home and sleep. I been chasin' this shit all weekend. I'm 'bout done."

Tone stuffed his hands in his sweatpants' pockets then puckered his lips in thought. When he spoke, his tone was harsh. "Oh, you just gonna roll out on me after I done caked your pockets?"

"See, I knew you was gonna think like that. I'm only tired, that's all - plus, copping' with you is dangerous. That's some serious shit you workin' on."

After a few seconds of silence, Tone pulled the gat from his waistband. "Here. You hold the gun then."

"I don't want that!" Daewoo protested. He pushed the 45 back at the teen. "All I'm tryin' to do is roll, my man."

Tone angrily tucked the gun away. "You tryin'a roll, huh?" He stepped within a foot of Daewoo and spoke with conviction. Each word echoing throughout the empty stairwell. "I thought we was gonna get a couple hoes and get our freak on, but no, your ass got the runs. I don't care what you think, Homeboy. This is just as much your case as it is mine. I just hope your ass remember one thing…" he pushed up on his toes and arched his face even closer, "I got somethin' on you. Dig? Whether or not I use it depends on you." Without another word, Tone stormed through the heavy, metal door.

Daewoo was stunned at possibly being implicated in the murders. He leaned his head back against the stairwell's cold wall and cursed his greed. For him, killing Tone was out of the question. He was a lot of things, but not a murderer. He grimaced at the thought of himself behind bars, in prison garbs, doing life. He also knew that regardless of how remorseful he felt about the murders, if he were nabbed, all that'll be considered would be: a life sentence or the death penalty. His remorse would mean zilch. His reasoning was simple. He could either leave or try regaining Tone's confidence so that he'll answer for his own actions. He dreaded the idea of spending more time with the psychopath but knew things couldn't stay as they were. Regretfully, he opened the door leading to the fifth floor. Daewoo stood silent and out of sight as he listens to Tone knock on an apartment door. He prayed Tone wouldn't turn this into another murder scene. He'd already made up his mind that, if Tone did, he was getting ghost. He listened carefully at the door opening, the door closing, then reopening. A paper-bag crumbling the door closing. He breathed easier.

Tone turned the bend and saw Daewoo standing there. "That's what I'm talkin' 'bout ol'head. Now, let's find a couple tricks."

Stoney's cell had been long ago dark, and the radio tunes eliminated. He'd ignored his celli's probing with a cold stare before flopping on his bunk and staring into oblivion. To him, nothing else mattered. Not even his own life. He'd always believed his mother would live far beyond her years. A single teardrop ran its course across his chiseled cheek, and subconsciously, he heard his mother's voice, soothing him, assuring him that everything will be all right. He closed his eyes to savor the moment. Eventually, he drifted into a pitiful sleep. Stoney awoke shivering and soaked in perspiration. His cellie had vanished, and the light and radio remained off. Only the muffled noises of inmates attending the norm squeezed through the metal cell door. Stoney laid, absorbing a heated argument over a pinochle game until an obese prison guard cracked his gate.

"Hightower! You got a visit," the guard boomed.

Stoney never questioned who his visits were. They were always either his father or his aunt Millie.

The visiting area was just beyond a barred checkpoint. Stoney was strip-searched and handed a pair of green khaki pants, a white V-neck shirt, and instructed to sit and wait for his visit to arrive.

The visiting room was airy and filled with an assortment of bright-colored rubber chairs. At the far end of the room, five vending machines stood stacked with precooked sandwiches, drinks, and junk-foods. The room's smiles, laughter, and tears brought life to an otherwise dreary day for prisoners. Some people conversed as they munched, while others sat content, quietly embracing one another, abstracted from their surroundings. And while adults tried catching up on one another's life, unruly children busied themselves climbing chairs, as frustrated moms gave chase - only to have the child scurry away once more. The room carried an infectious mood that flowed from one individual to another. It gave a prisoner some gratification to know that regardless of what hardships life presents, he wasn't alone - something every inmate cherished before returning to the loneliness and despair of jailing.

Stoney found it difficult to control his own emotions with love being displayed. He looked on as a mother and son embraced. The image of his mother in a casket surrounded with wreaths entered his thoughts, and impatiently he chaperoned the visitors' entrance in hopes of being Milton Hightower descended from the visiting room's narrow entrance. He stood a huge six-three, 320 pounds, and had played football for Benjamin Franklin High School. Several colleges had taken an interest in him until he and two teammates decided to spice an evening with alcohol. One teammate had swiped a gallon of vodka from his parents along with the Trans Am keys. Two hours later, firefighters were feverishly cutting Milton from the back seat - minus half a kneecap and a cracked collar-bone. Milton's teammates weren't as lucky. Both were crushed during the tractor trailer's impact. To this day, Milton regretted his decision and carried a limp. Milton understood the sum of Stoney's dilemma. He, too, had been raised in projects and have been faced with continuous setbacks. It'd been a struggle for him to instill positive influences in Stoney's life. His divorce from Candy had ensured that - forcing him into the role of part-time father. When Stoney was fourteen, Milton had recognized his son's delinquency and suggested the boy stay with him. He'd considered transferring Stoney's schooling then rendered against it, sensing that school wasn't the problem, 13th Street was. Regardless of how often he forbade Stoney from venturing around Saigon, he couldn't enforce it without forbidding him form visiting his mother. After two years of "I'm done with you" speeches, Stoney had thrust even deeper into licentiousness. Milton hoped Stoney's first taste of prison upstate would serve as a wake-up call.

The two men met at the center of the room and embraced for a full minute.

"Come on, Son, sit down," Milton coaxed, recalling his own anguish when he'd lost his mother.

"Millie told you already, huh?"

"I'm sorry, Son."

Teary-eyed, Stoney leaned forward, elbows on thighs, and palmed a huge fist. "Do they know who did it?" he sniffed.

"No. I don't think so…at least they haven't said anything to us. Ryan's got the case."

"Ryan?"

"Mmmm…hmm. That's what they say." Stoney pushed back in his chair.

"You want something to eat?" Milton asked.

"I'm all right. I ain't got much of a appetite."

"I hope you plan on eating something. No sense in starving yourself."

"How's Aunt Millie?" Stoney asked.

"She's O.K. A lotta crying, but she'll pull through."

Stoney looked solemnly at his father. "You know, Dad, I never ever thought about losing a parent like this. It hurts not being able to say goodbye."

Milton dropped an arm around Stoney's shoulder. "Listen, Son," he whispered. "I found out, when your grandmother passed, that certain things can't be controlled. Life is one. I know you're going through hell, and being stuck here don't help much, but you gotta dig deep to find strength to maintain. I don't want you up here, stressing yourself out." Milton's eyes became serious.

"I'll be all right," Stoney drawled. "You just make sure Ryan stay on top of the case."

"I'm sure he'll do everything he can. He knows how important this is to us."

Two hours later, Stoney was lain on his bunk, racking his brain for answers. He thought of all the stickup men he knew who targeted drug dealers. The list was long, but none would've crossed him like this. His thoughts wandered to Ryan, handling the case. Although Ryan was also familiar with the neighborhood stickup men, it wasn't enough to assure Stoney that the case wouldn't eventually be swept under the rug. "I'll find you," he mumbled solemnly. "I'll find you."

Chapter Two

Man send that bitch steppin', she fuckin' up my high with that skitsin' shit!"

"Don't even worry 'bout it," Daewoo said firmly. "That's just her high."

Tone glanced around wildly. "I don't care what her high is. You coulda came up with somebody better than her."

"Shit," Daewoo drawled, "she might skits, but she can suck a bullet out a rifle."

Both Tone and Daewoo laughed as they watched the poppy eyed girl search the floor for cocaine. Her skin was burnt chocolate, giving her an older look than her twenty-five years. The hard lines disappeared from around her mouth when she smiled. Short and thin, she appeared undernourished but still attractive - even with her boyish frame.

Besides poking around on the floor, she also darted back and forth to the window, rattling Tone's nerves.

"Daewoo, man, on the serious note, you better calm that hoe down or, I swear, I'm a blast her ass."

Daewoo believed him and summoned her over. "Girl, dig this," he said. "You are blowing my man high. You gotta chill 'fore he put your ass out, all right?"

With pursed lips she purred, "Mmmm…hmm," still surveying the littered floor for pebbles. "I know, Boop, but this coke got my pussy all wet. I can't keep still."

"Oh, shit!" Tone shrieked. You keep talkin' like that, you might get all this coke."

"No way," Daewoo cut in. "You didn't even want her around a minute ago. Plus, I'm first. When I'm done, you can get down."

Tone struck two matches as he spoke. "It's cool. I ain't frontin' on sloppy seconds, all I want is some face anyway."

"Me, too." Daewoo trekked to the window and peered onto the street.

"Is the cops still out there?" Tone asked. "I don't see none."

Tone looked for himself. "So, what now?" he asked. "Ain't this what you been waitin' on?"

Daewoo's objective had been to establish a sense of sovereignty and to separate himself from Tone as soon as possible.

For a moment, he was tempted to stay. He was somewhat enjoying himself but knew he'd better put distance between them. "Yeah, I guess so," he sighed, not wanting to sound too anxious.

"Where you goin'" Tone asked.

"I'm takin' my black ass home. That's where I was goin' before… well…you know."

"You takin' her too?" Tone nodded toward the woman.

"Nah, you can get down."

Tone stepped closer. "You know we gotta get together later, right?"

"For what?"

"For what? To get our stories straight. Just in case." "I'm not saying' shit," Daewoo replied with gusto. "I'm denying this shit to the grave. In fact, I don't even know your ass."

Tone smiled, satisfied. "That's all the better," he stated, "but still meet me at Scorpio's tonight."

"Whatever," Daewoo muttered before heading to the boarded entrance. He peered over his shoulder to see Tone hover over the perched woman fumbling with his sweatpants. For a second, Daewoo regretted paying the woman up-front and not collecting. His leaving subsided any real disappointment. Once he stepped into the hall, he felt as if all his burdens were lifted.

"Shhittt. Mmmm…yeah, that's right, suck it, Baby," Tone gasped as his body responded to the warmth of her mouth. Her moans added to his pleasure, creating an enormous wave of ecstasy throughout him. He remembered Daewoo praising the woman's talents as another spasm caused his toes to curl inside his Fila sneakers. He grabbed the woman's head with both hands and pushed deeper into her throat. "Oh, girl, don't stop. Yeah, just like that," he coaxed, knowing she needed none. He was near his sexual peek when she allowed him to slip from her mouth.

"Mmmm, Daddy," she cooed, massaging him in her

palms. "You like this?" she asked. "I bet nobody ever made you feel this way." She planted small, loving kisses the length of his shaft. "I know where the coke came from," she whispered, peering up at Tone with glazed pupils.

"What?" Tone managed.

She continued massaging him. "I know where the coke came from," she repeated.

"What the fuck you talkin' 'bout!" Tone snapped. He pulled his penis from her hands and tucked it away.

She glared at him indignant, as if she'd been robbed.

"Don't even front," she sassed. "I ain't stupid." She stood and rolled her eyes. "First of all, I saw you almost run outta Saigon right before I heard about Candy getting stuck-up."

"Girl, you trippin'."

"Listen, boo, I don't care what y'all done did, all I want is a little somethin' for myself."

"Bitch, I don't know shit about no damn Candy. You better step the fuck off talkin' that crazy shit," Tone barked. He eased to where his sweat-jacket masked the huge 45. As Tone neared his jacket, a transformation occurred. His features were solid, and his cold, brown eyes gleamed dangerously. He was shocked this whore would try shaking him down. He snatched the gun from under the jacket and faced her. Everything was a blur besides her frightened expression. Before she could utter a protest, the trigger was pulled. The gunshot illuminated the room's darkness, and before the grayish-blue flash diminished, her slim body slumped to the floor.

Tone stepped over the woman's body, gathered his

coke, and left the apartment. As far as he was concerned, he'd done what was needed. He hit the stairwell running, regretting she didn't finish the blow-job before opening her big fuckin' mouth.

"Barry!" Benita Maxwell hollered. She quickly dried her hands on a dish towel and roved the small apartment.

"Yes?" a child answered.

She sighed, relieved her seven-year old son was in his room and not in the building's hallway. "Nothing, baby," she called back. "I just wanna make sure you're here." She reeled off a string of obscenities while dialing 911. "The same old shit. Damn dope dealers shooting all over the place. Ain't got respect for no-damn-body."

"9-1-1 emergency," a female's voice sang.

"Hello, Police?"

"Please hold."

She pulled the receiver from her ear and gave it a disgusting look. A full minute later, she was connected.

"Police Department," a man boomed.

"This is Benita Maxwell. I live at 1212 Fitzwater, apartment 9-G."

"What can I do for you, Ms. Maxwell?"

"You can send someone to find out who's shooting in the hallway."

"Are you sure it was a gunshot you heard?"

"It sure as hell ain't Fourth of July!" she spat.

"No, Ma'am, it's not, but I still need to ask."

She paced the floor as she spoke. "No. I'm not sure, and I'm not about to go out there to find out either."

"What's your apartment again?" the voice asked.

"9-G!" she barked.

"O.K., we'll send someone over."

"Mm…hm. I'll be here," she said crisply, before slamming down the phone receiver.

Ryan was exiting Saigon when he remembered the surveillance camera aimed at its entrance. The probability of the murderer being filmed was intriguing.

The morning blushed a blue sky and sunshine. Even at a bit past ten, residents huddled to mimic words about the killings. Some clutched pampered children in their arms, not bothering to clothe the child in their haste to get the freshest gossip. There wasn't even much to see. A few police cruisers on pavements and a K-9 vehicle summoned to search Candy's apartment for drugs.

Ryan minced over to a group of housing guards and eyeballed a nameplate. He chose a rookie. "Officer Murrell, how you doing?" Ryan asked.

Each officer turned to him. "I'm fine," Murrell answered.

Ryan flipped open his worn leather wallet and revealed his badge. "Can I speak to you for a second?"

"Sure. What's up?"

Murrell was broad shouldered with a lot of mustache. Ryan steered him to a slow walk. "I'm hoping you can answer something for me."

"I'll try."

"Can you tell me if the cameras in these units work?"

"Sure. They work…at least…most of the time."

"All night?"

"I believe so, but you have to change the tapes."

"I asked because I can't recall them ever being there." "That's because they've only been installed a month ago."

Ryan stopped walking. "Who was on duty last night?" he asked.

Murrell thought for a moment. "That would be Dokes."

"Is he still around?"

"I don't think so. I just started my shift and haven't had time to

"O.K. O.K…," Ryan interrupted with a halting hand and a smile. "I understand. Believe me, I'm not trying to be hard-assed."

The officer smiled, spreading his thick mustache across his face.

"Just a couple more things," Ryan insisted. "Do you know where the tapes are?"

"I sure do. In a metal file cabinet over at headquarters."

Ryan pulled a personalized card from his pocket and gave it to the officer. "I'd appreciate if you'd get last night's tapes to me immediately."

"No problem. Is that it?" Ryan surveyed the area.

"Yeah, for now.

After Murrell rejoined the other officers, Ryan looked over the plaza once more. The once manicured greenswards that had encircled each of the four high rises, now lay thirsty, displaying huge blotches of dirt while weathered buildings and ancient homes were now only crumbs of expectations. Ryan shook his head, dismayed, and watched two ashy-legged boys haul tail into a Korean owned store. He wondered if "Black America" would ever become industrial minded - or, would blacks continue throughout their tethered existence park themselves into back seats of progress and accept what others extended to them.

A sweltering sun had cooked the Plymouth's vinyl seating. Ryan turned up the air and allowed it to circulate before pulling from the curb. He contemplated an early lunch at home. Another depressing thought. He loathed Deitra's decision to spend time apart - their first separation in their eleven-year marriage. Unaware of their parents' division, the children seemed to welcome the change of pace. Usually, he'd call before visiting, but today, he found himself heading in that direction.

The drive across Parkway had been short - credit Ryan's swallowing memories of courting Deitra. They'd attended the same elementary and high schools, and she'd made him earn their first date by squashing hordes of invites with polite smiles.

By tenth grade, Ryan had begun wondering if she'd any interests besides school. Soon after, he discovered her evenings, almost always, consisted of babysitting children. Children had seemed to be Deitra's closest friends. By senior year, he'd nearly given up on her until one morning, during homeroom, he asked her out, again. He'd thought she was joking when she'd accepted and informed him of her ten o'clock curfew. The rest was magical - until he met her iron-fisted father. Back then, Charlie Garnett had been all spit-shine and seriousness, having served seventeen years in the Navy. At Ryan and Delta's engagement, he'd pitched a fit; whereas Deitra's mother couldn't've been more delighted and cried a rainstorm at the wedding. Ryan wondered what she'd seen in his father-in-law and asked her. She replied," He grows on you." She also had mentioned something about men in uniforms. He'd let it go at that.

Before the Plymouth was parked, Ryan spotted Mira, his oldest child, bolt from the house towards the car. Her hair was pulled into a single ponytail, and her thin arms flailed wildly as if she were in a state of hysteria. She was nearing thirteen and just beginning to fill her clothes. She clasped her father's waist as he swung close the car door. "Hey, Dad," she greeted, her voice muffled against his abdomen.

"Aye, Pumpkin. How's my baby?" he asked lovingly.

"Fine. What took you so long to come see us?"

"Working," he stated. He pried the child form him.

"You ain't eating all grand mom's food, are you?"

"No," she giggled.

"That's good." lie gathered her next to his huge frame as they walked to the house. He noticed her quietness.

"What's wrong?"

Her face was serious. "I'm ready to go home."

"Well, did you tell your mom that?"

The girl frowned. "No."

"Why not?"

"Cause, she be trippin' out. You know she's still mad at you."

"It's upset with me," Ryan corrected. "And why do

you think she's upset anyway?"

"I don't know. She's always crying."

"Where is she?"

"In the kitchen with Grand mom."

"How about telling her I'm out here?"

The girl stopped and gave him a disappointed look. "You're not coming in?"

"Not right now, Pumpkin. I want to talk to your mom first."

Her small face brightened. "O.K.," she yelled, sprinting into the house.

Ryan winced at the afternoon sun as he leaned against his in-laws Ford Diplomat. Deitra emerged from the house garbed in gray sweats. Even homely, Ryan thought, she was gorgeous. A green-eyed redbone with small, pinkish lips. Her grandfather, a Caucasian, accounted for her eyes and complexion, but her well endowment was inherited from her mother, who's African American and Dutch.

"Look what the cat dragged in," she announced. She planted one foot forward and folded her arms, genie-like. "So, what do we owe this pleasure to?" she added, her neck swiveling like a cobra poised to strike.

Ryan sensed she wasn't in the best mood. "I thought I'd drop by to admire your big, beautiful smile."

"Mm…hm," she hummed, eyes locked with her husband's, seriousness pasted across her face. "You didn't seem concerned with my 'big, beautiful smile' when I was home."

"Aw, come on, Dee. Let's not go there. It's already been a hectic morning. I just wanted to say hello."

"Mm…hm," she hummed again. She shifted her weight to her other leg. Her arms remained folded.

"Now, Dee," Ryan said matter of fact, "I know you don't believe I don't want you home?"

"No. I'm not saying that at all. What I'm saying is that your responsibilities at home are far more important than your fantasy job, and you need a reality check."

Ryan felt an argument erupting. An argument he'd no chance of winning. He went straight for her weakness. Hearing him beg. He stepped within a foot of her with puppy-dog eyes and peered down at her 5'7 frame. "Dee, I know I've been inconsiderate. I was wrong and regret those decisions. I do love you…very much. You know that don't you?"

She didn't answer.

Ryan knew she was getting through to her and went into an even deeper spiel. "Honey, since you've been gone, I've realized that my family means more to me than any job. I'm terribly sorry for putting you through that. I guess what I'm saying is that…I have some vacation time save up, and…well, I'm hoping, while the kids are still out of school, we can take a trip somewhere - Disneyland perhaps or somewhere…as a family…start all over - and…"

"Ryan," she interrupted, having heard enough. "What's wrong with you? You just don't get it, do you? She shook her head, disbelieving. As if a man as intelligent as Ryan could be so naive. "It's more than you working late. And it'll take a lot more than a trip to Disneyland to fix things."

Ryan's earlier confidence became dejection. "Fix

what?" he complained.

Her eyes were pleading. "You alienating us from your life, your mood swings, your continuous cancellations of everything important to our children. Your never at home. And what about me, Ryan? Don't you think I need my man home instead of who-knows-where?" Her arms flailed as she spoke, and tears dripped from her eyes.

Ryan moved in to console her.

"No. Get off of me," she protested, pushing him away.

"Baby, I'm so sorry," Ryan said apologetically. "But you didn't have to leave to get me to change."

"Oh, no? Then how else am I supposed to show you how much you're hurting us?"

"Dee, if I'd known how serious you were about this, I'd have changed. In fact, I'm still willing to. Don't you think you're hurting us by leaving?"

She wiped a tear with a delicate hand. "I'm not going to argue with you, Ryan."

"I don't want to argue either," he conceded. "Just think about what I said, O.K.? If not for me, then for the children. I know they'd like to be home. "Their argument ended when their ten-year-old son pulled his five-year-old sister through the door.

Ryan scooped up his daughter and ruffled the boy's curly hair. "Aye, Shorty. How are you?" Ryan asked the boy.

"I'm not short," he objected.

"You're right. And I bet your jump shot still falls left. Am I right?"

The boy blushed and nodded a simple yes.

Ryan noticed his wife's gander and turned to her. "Just think about what I said, O.K.?"

"You plan on cornin' in this house an' saying' hello?" Betty Garnett's husky voice spun everyone's head toward the house.

"Of course, I am," Ryan answered.

She held the screen door open as they all filed into the home.

Ryan pecked his mother-in-law's cheek then whispered, "Talk to her, will you?"

Betty Garnett had once been a Copa Dancer. And still, at fifty-six, she was a compact five-three with extremely stunning legs. With her slightly tanned skin, vernal eyes, and full lips. Ryan considered her a very handsome woman as well as a huge flirt. And shamefully, on several occasions, he'd found himself wondering what she was like in the sack. She'd cornered Ryan on a florid Victorian sofa, in a living room filled with ceramic knickknacks and throw pillows. When Deitra vanished into the kitchen, and the children were beside themselves with Nintendo games, Ryan followed up on his earlier question. "Did you talk to Dee," he asked.

"No," she answered, slipping into a Southern drawl. She sat opposite her son-in-law. "Now you know 'dere's no talkin' ta' 'dat 'dere girl where yall's troubles concerned. I done already told her ta' take her butt on home."

"And what did she say?"

Betty threw her head back and laughed. "You know what she said. She tol' me ta' stay outta it, like she always does - when I can't see how I can, the way she run 'round here poutin' and carrin' on like she does."

Ryan was pleased the separation was taking its toll on Deitra as well. "I wouldn't worry much more, Mom. I think Dee and the kids will be out of your hair soon."

"Hell, I don't care 'bout 'dat," she remarked. "I welcome 'da company. It's more that 'dat ol' fart's been."

Ryan looked over the room. "Where is Charlie anyway?"

"Down in 'dat dag on basement fixin' somethin' as always.

"He act like he don't know it's another world up here."

Ryan wondered if the old man's fishing rod was the only rod needing fixing. "Yeah, the kids told me. I guess I better go down and say hello, huh?"

She stood up and yarned. "Mm…hm. I can already hear him bitchin' if you don't, 'siderin' he been hollerin' 'bout 'da noise an' all."

Ryan muscled a smile and headed for the basement.

Both white officers exited their cruiser, palms steady above unsnapped gun holsters and qualms about entering the housing project. There were too many windows, and just as many crazies just itching to squeeze off a pop-shot at some white cop. Fortunately, they made it into the building's lobby safely, but the elevator ride to the 9th floor was just as horrid. Minutes ago, they'd received orders to respond to a complaint of shots being fired. When the elevator door opened, both uniforms had their weapons drawn. They searched the small hallway and found nothing. Breathing easier, they shoved their snub-noses back into their holsters and searched out apartment 9-G. Officer Landers, a burly man wearing wire-frame glasses, rapt loudly on the door.

"Who is it?" a child's voice cried.

Bogwell, a tall scrawny man, talked mostly in these situations. "The Police!" he answered.

Seconds later, Benita Maxwell was at the door. "Who is it?"

"Police, Ma'am."

The door opened the length of the safety chain. Benita Maxwell's face peeked through the crack. "Well," she chided. "It took yall long enough." She closed the door and removed the chain.

When she reopened it, Bogwell spoke "You called about the shots?"

"Yes, I did." She allowed them into the apartment.

Bogwell wasn't enjoying the woman's dander. "Miss Maxwell, did you observe anyone in the hallway after you heard the shots?"

"It was only one shot. And, no, I didn't go into the hall.

"How about neighbors? Any of them go into the hall?"

She gave Bogwell an irritated look. "Now, how would I know something like that?" she spat, then seemed to regain her poise before speaking again. "Look, I heard the shot, so I called you. I never went to the door…before or after. O.K.?"

Bogwell eyed his partner for answers then realized Landers was busily scanning the apartment. He decided to appeal to her decency. "Miss Maxwell, I'd appreciate if you'd just bear with me for a few moments. I'm sorry, but I do have to ask these questions."

"Yeah, whatever," she hissed with a hand twist at the wrist.

After a few more questions, Bogwell closed his notepad and headed for the door.

"So, that's it?" she asked.

"For now." Landers spoke for the first time. "If you happen to hear anything else, please, don't hesitate to call."

"Believe me, I won't," she shot back, catching the sarcasm in the flatfoot's words.

Bogwell smiled. He, too, had caught the irritation in his partner's words.

Benita Maxwell followed the cops out into the hall. While she and Landers sparred goodbyes, Bogwell ogled the abandoned tenement next door. The alignment of the plywood covering the entrance was off. His suspicions flared and he grabbed his partner's arm and nodded in its direction.

Landers quickly picked up on his partner's suspicions.

"Can you step back into the apartment, Ms. Maxwell?" Landers asked. He gave her a small shove backward.

"For what?" she asked stubbornly.

"Just for a minute," he retorted, this time insisting.

She saw the officers draw their weapons and decided to obey. Nervously, the officers posted on each side of the entrance. They held their guns high, gripped tightly, while Bogwell, with a free hand, inched the board free from its base. He signaled for his partner to follow suit, and with one quick yank, they sent the board crashing against the opposite wall.

Both men were wide-eyed as they hurriedly pointed their weapons into the hovel. Already beads of sweat formed noticeably over their brows as both cops entered the hole ghost faced.

The apartment was illuminated just enough that, in only a few steps inward, Bogwell spotted the sprawled body on the floor. "Check the rest of the place," Bogwell whispered as he kneeled over the body, lain face down, in a pool of blood. He holstered his gun and checked her wrist for a pulse.

"It's all clear," Landers announced. He squatted next to his partner and saw Bogwell's concern. "How is she?" he asked.

"Still alive," Bogwell responded, "but we need an ambulance fast."

Chapter Three

The living room's lights were dimmed just enough to obscure the tiny tribe of inebriates parked beneath much-needed drinks. Some were permitted to pass the band-aid bar separating the house. That privilege was for V.I.P. customers and boarders. Beasty, an ex-con, was house lady at "Scorpios" and stressed it adamantly when rowdies got out of line. She was a stocky dike, in her late forties, with a long, curved scar be- hind her left ear stretching to a stout chin. All her front teeth were missing. This influenced her to cover her mouth when she cackled. Beasty kept the place dark to avoid the drunken faces. To her, her business was necessary - slow, but sure - at least the selling of alcohol phase of it. She also provided anything from marijuana to heroin to her more dedicated customers, but on most days, her speakeasy was a place where vagabonds could drink when most legal establishments closed for the night.

While Beasty busied herself with a *special* customer, the living room reeked of raw bickering. Today's wrangling erupted over the earlier killings in Saigon. Everyone had heard of Candy's fate and drew their own conclusions.

"No doubt about it. It was a stick-up," one old man slurred, shuffling to the bar for a refill of Thunderbird.

"I tol' her ass 'bout sellin' 'dat shit, 'dat time 'a night!" a stone-faced woman coughed around her Pall Mall. "She had all day ta' make 'er little money, but nooo, 'dat bitch gotta sell 'dat shit all night long. If you ask me, she got just what 'da fuck she was askin' for."

"Aw, shut the fuck up, Pat. Ain't nobody ask you, cause your ass don't know what to say outta your filthy ass mouth," the old man hollered over his shoulder while Beasty refilled his cup.

"Nigga, I know enough not ta' be sellin' no damn crack 'dat time 'a mornin'."

"Well, you can say what you want. Don't nobody deserve to be killed over no little bit 'a coke," the old timer grumbled as he retreated to his chair, wine-cup full.

In a corner chair, nursing a can of Old English, Daewoo listened to the pair cross swords. He wondered if the police had uncovered any clues leading back to him. Confident they hadn't, he settled in the cushioned armchair and rested his head back. He'd made it to Scorpio's where he and Tone were supposed to meet to collaborate their alibis. Regardless what story they'd conjure up, Daewoo knew he'd never stick to it. Why should he, he thought. He felt no loyalty to Tone, whose cold-bloodedness indicated he'd've just as easily killed him as well. Daewoo hadn't yet slept as he'd hoped to; although, he tried. Unfortunately, he'd been denied access into Saigon because he'd lacked proper authorization. He felt like kicking his own ass for not getting Trina to add his name to the visiting list. He recalled the face of seriousness that had greeted him when he'd entered Saigon.

"What apartment?" a housing guard had commanded.

Even before the man had spoken, Daewoo had felt his chest tighten with nervousness. He grabbed the inner door's handle and gave a shocked look at being stopped.

"What's your name?"

"'David Stokes."

The stone-faced guard searched his manifest. "You're not listed. You visiting?"

"I live here."

"Not according to this list."

Daewoo explained how it was his children's mother place, all the while, feeling as if his heart would burst from fear if someone shouted, "Grab him!" Out of sheer desperation, he controlled his trembling and gave the guard a solemn look. "Sir, I'm not lyin'. I live here."

"Not today, Buddy," the man said dismissingly.

Outside of Saigon, imprisoned by the noon heat, Daewoo slumped onto one of three benches in the plaza too tired and too afraid to argue with the guard. To draw heat to himself would prove insane. He eyed a toddler wobble behind its father and thought of his own mud-rats. For two months, he'd not given Trina any monetary support for their two children. Maybe it was time, he thought, as he peeled two hundred from his bankroll and headed towards 1241 building.

Daewoo ignored trying to enter 1241 building; instead, he called Trina from the lobby's payphone. Her voice was sultry over the line, even though her questioning stung.

"What's wrong? You locked up?" she asked accusingly.

"No. Ain't nobody locked up. Stop sayin' shit like that. I'm in the lobby. I got some money for you."

"Boy, stop playing," she scolded.

"I ain't playin'. Meet me in the lobby." He listened as she sucked her teeth.

"I'll be down," she puffed petulantly, then hung up.

Daewoo replaced the receiver and checked the coin slot. He couldn't blame Trina for her suspiciousness. Since the worsening of his cocaine addiction, his generosity hasn't amounted to much. He'd never treasured the easy money he'd come by and had made it a point to constantly break Trina off. That was when he'd hustled all day building a bankroll. Now, after nearly every sting, he'd break his neck to the cop-man. Although he smoked, he still considered himself a player - as did many other smokers, who globetrotted cross-country, hustling various con games such as: "Three Card Monty," "Pigeon Drop," "Top and the Ball," "Slumming," and a host of others. Daewoo's forte was the "Slum Game," and he took extreme pride in taking the game to a new level, whether it be junk jewelry stamped 14K or fake drugs. But now, with his drug habit a priority, it was a struggle to hustle throughout one full day.

Trina emerged swaying big-boned hips beneath a simple, ankle-length black striped summer dress with a high thigh slit down each side. Her skin was a natural deep brown, but during the summer months, it turned an attractive chocolate to highlight her bright ebony eyes. Her hair, permed short and waved, was decorated with specks of golden glitter, and with each stride taken, a meaty chocolate thigh hung teasingly from a slit.

It's been days since they've seen one another and both casted curious glances.

"Girl, look at you lookin' all good," Daewoo teased. "Where you 'bout to go?"

"Don't play with me," she warned, enjoying the compliment none-the-less. "I ain't going nowhere."

Daewoo smirked. "Yeah right."

Her eyes narrowed. "You said you had something for me?"

"No. I got somethin' for the kids."

She crossed her arms, offended. "Do it matter, Daewoo? Ain't like they can spend it their damn self - plus, we a family, remember?"

"Yeah, *I remember*. I hope you ain't tryin'a make me feel any worse?"

"Maybe that's what your ass need to get you to leave that shit alone - somebody to make you feel bad."

He knew she was right. "I told you I would, didn't I?"

"About a thousand times."

"I'm serious, Trina. Why you think I'm givin' you this?"

She held out a limp palm until he filled it with bills.

Without a glance, she pocketed it, more interested in the gratified expression on Daewoo's face.

"Just make sure you get 'em somethin' nice," he blurted.

"Don't worry, I don't do drugs," she replied nastily, ticked at his accusation.

"Why you gotta go there. I try to do somethin' nice for a change, and you still don't appreciate it."

Her eyes roamed the sky for answers then back to Daewoo.

"You expect me to thank you for doing something for your kids? That's your responsibility. You need to try harder."

"You right, Trina. My bad. I'm sorry."

"Yes, you are."

"There you go again. But you know what…I ain't even gonna argue with you. All I wanna know is when you comin' home?"

"When you get it together."

"Well, I guess that's never, huh?" he chuckled morbidly.

Trina shot him a dirty look. "Daewoo, you done lost your mind. "

"Girl, I'm only jokin'," he hurriedly said, realizing that the joke was a bad one.

"I'll tell your kids you said hi," she threw over her shoulder before turning and skating away.

His eyes locked on the swaying curves of her rump until she entered the building. "I'll be damn," he grumbled, realizing he'd forgotten he needed her to get into Saigon.

On a marred bench outside of 1241 building, Daewoo wolfed down a cheese hoagie, sour-cream chips, and a Welch's grape soda. He wondered how long it'd be until the next meal. He was already contemplating getting high, and with his pockets itching with cash and cocaine, he knew it'd be a while before he'd pause to eat again. He was a regular at

Laney's. After paying the two-vial toll, he was provided a room and a straight shooter. The straight shooter was small. A six-inch glass stem, with thin, tangled, and burned copper-wire loaded at one end to hold the melted cocaine. The other end was used for inhaling. On the way over, Daewoo had stopped for beer and matches.

He made a shovel of the matchbook cover then ripped away the matchsticks in pairs. After packing the stem with coke, he took a long drag from the stem, choking. Back smoke threatening to escape his lungs. Not until he exhaled a mammoth smoke cloud did the effects of the hit seize him. His eyes ballooned from their sockets and his heart raced wildly. With a trembling hand, he clumsily laid the stem on a ruined nightstand and quickly downed a long swig of Old English 800. In cessation, he took hits as the room thickened with the pungent smoke; his breaths came in short, rapid increments. Beads of sweat dripped from his bald head as his phobia began showing its horrible face. Images of angry policemen surrounding the crack house had captured his thoughts, and he scolded himself for not buying enough beer to tame them. He peeked outside, from behind drawn shades, knowing he'd need weed or more beer to control his paranoia. While high, he'd never felt comfortable around people. He'd assume everyone he'd pass would know he was high and laugh at him. Finally, having had enough torturing, he gathered his mess, secured the remaining coke deep in his shoe, and left.

Beasty's loud cackling brought Daewoo from his stupor. He'd come to Scorpio's to sedate his high and to meet Tone, not to get drunk. He sat his fifth can of Old

English on the floor and tried lifting himself from the chair. Wearily, he slumped back into the seat, exhausted from the three-day binge. Once his eyes shut and his head fell back against the chair cushion, he was out cold.

"I honestly could not estimate the duration of her coma, Detective. You never can tell in these circumstances," Doctor Hughes explained. "Unfortunately," she continued, "at this point, we're helpless. But don't worry, Detective, as soon as something significant develops, I'll notify your department."

"I'd appreciate that, Doc," Ryan declared, settling in an armchair outside the hospital room's door. He had eagerly made the drive to Pennsylvania Hospital shortly after his visit with the children. He was still uncertain of Deitra's intentions, but certain the visit had achieved its purpose, which was, expressing the broken-heartedness due to their separation.

The call had come at his desk, where he hid enjoying the air conditioning, salvaged from outside's blistering summer heat. He'd been reviewing interviews retrieved from patrolmen who'd questioned some of Saigon's residents. He was then ready for his own interrogating after allowing word to spread around the projects. Usually, someone wounded up seeing or hearing news about someone possessing an unusual amount of money or drugs.

With a forefinger, Ryan had punched the office line's blinking light. "Detective Page," he answered.

"Ryan, how's it coining?"

"Not too good, Captain."

"Mm…hm. Well, maybe this'll pave the way a bit.

There was another shooting. This time in Twelve-Twelve. A girl."

Ryan sat back, frustrated. "And this is supposed to do what…make my day better?"

Plummer chuckled. "Of course not, but maybe this will. The bullet matches the Montross'."

Ryan's eyebrows had rose a full inch. "You kidding?"

"I kid not."

"What about prints?"

"Sure. They found plenty. No help though, active crack house and all."

"Where's the body?"

"In Pennsylvania. Get this. She's still alive."

Ryan had surged with excitement. "I'm on it," he'd stated.

"I'm sure you are. Keep me informed" Plummer had asked.

That call had occurred thirty minutes ago. Now, optimistic outside of the woman's hospital room, Ryan wondered what she knew to deserve a bullet. He'd hoped she'd be capable of identifying her shooter. After two hours of waiting, he issued his card to the head nurse before leaving. Tomorrow he'd begin a second, more depth investigation.

No sooner than the traffic light turned green, the black BMW roared across the intersection of 13th & Christian Streets. Tone's mood was sleek as he pushed the stolen

Beemer through the ghetto's pitted streets. Three times he's passed the corner crap game. And like most teenage car thieves from the hood, he made certain the hip-hop music was heard before the car was seen cruising by.

After a half-hour of cruising the neighborhood out of boredom, he glanced in the rearview mirror and cursed the police car closing in on him. Instinctively, he sat tall, lowered the music, and slowed to a halt at a stop sign he'd previously ignored. He reached beneath the car seat for the 45. Tone had heard the stories of adult prison and wanted no parts of it. Repeatedly, he'd promised himself he'd hold his court on the streets. To him, dying wasn't an issue, just a fact which everyone had a certainty of experiencing. He relaxed under the 45's heft, finding comfort along with a surge of power and pleasure in knowing he could control life with one flinch of a finger. He pulled from the stop sign and turned onto a small street. When the patrol car followed, he gritted his teeth, acknowledging the tags were probably being traced. He'd changed them earlier, of course, but he also suspected he'd be stopped regardless and quickly headed toward Broad Street, an inter- section wide enough to begin the chase.

Behind the Beemer, Officer Rivera received word that the car's license plate was clean. He adjusted his seat and tried for a glimpse of the driver. As an experienced cop, he under- stood, as in most cases, license plates were switched to avoid heat. Trusting his instincts, he continued his pursuit in hopes of the driver doing something to warrant a stop. If not, he'd pull alongside the Beemer on Broad Street, eye the driver, then make his decision whether to stop the vehicle. With the thought of jail lurking, Tone tried to avoid the mistake of panicking. If matters worsened, he'd hit a small street near the projects and run for it with his gun blazing. No way, he thought, would he allow himself to be caught. As Tone turned into the Broad Street traffic, he eyed his rearview. The police car was still there with its left turn-signal indicating a lane change. Tone's grip tightened around the pistol as he checked his blindside for traffic. There was none. When the police car pulled alongside the BMW's trunk, Tone signaled and faded opposite the cruiser onto a gas station's parking lot. He watched the angry expression on the cop's face as the man's head swirled backward, and the busy traffic carried him off. Tone chuckled. Now he'd have to get rid of the car. He was sure one of the project's dope dealers would buy the Beemer for a few c-notes, file down its serial number, and claim it. Tone could care less what happened after he was paid. The pain sake would lie with the buyer and the smuck who'd parked in an area notorious for car thefts.

Chang's Deli housed its usual dealers chatting around three booths. Others watched for customers through a huge storefront window, lettered bold and black: **"CHANG'S DELI."** All eyes turned to Tone as he parked the car out front. Tone sat for a few seconds nodding to the latest Tupac CD. He knew what effect the maneuver would have on the impressionable dealers. What they were witnessing is that which they hustle for – the *American Dream*.

As expected, two dealers exited the store. One extremely tall, lean, and sporting a colorful Hilfiger sweatshirt. A thin, gold chain hung from his neck.

Tone saw that the guy was doped up. He took notice

of the second dealer. A round male draped in all black.

The taller dealer stopped and admired the car. "Yo. Wass up, Dog?"

Tone exited the car with Tupac still blaring. He stood next to both dealers and admired the car as well. He had to admit that the music made the car more enticing. "You like?" he answered.

"Hell yeah," Shorty blurted.

"How much?"

"Three bills and it's yours."

"I guess you ain't got no papers, huh?" the dopehead replied.

"Nah, ain't no papers, but I do got keys." Tone jingled the keys around his forefinger.

"Where did it come from?"

"Northside."

Both dealers glanced at the other.

"Hold up a sec," Shorty mumbled before the pair stumbled back into the deli.

Tone's been on the flipside of a buy before. He reached beneath the car seat for his gun, making certain the dealers saw him stuff it into his waistband. He leaned against the merchandise and folded his arms. A soft "yes" escaped him as he watched, through the window, an older guy flip some bills onto the table. Tone sensed a deal would be made. He readied himself as they re-emerged from the deli. Shorty palmed the doe, but Stretch's lips were moving.

"Dig this, Youngin'," Stretch said. "How long you had the car?"

"Two days."

Stretch glanced at the ride then suspiciously at Tone. "You sure that's it?"

"Yeah, that's it," Tone lied, knowing he had the car over four days.

Slim stepped forward. "If anything's fucked up 'bout this whip, besides being stolen, I hope you ain't holdin' back."

"Ain't nothin' else to be said."

"I get to test drive it, right?" Stretch asked.

Tone smiled. All you gotta do is pay me. I'll be here when you get back."

"It's cool. I'ma take your word. I seen you around here before."

Shorty nodded in agreement.

Tone wished he could say the same. "So, what's up? We doin' business?"

Stretch nodded to Shorty, who forked over three crispy hundred-dollar bills.

Tone pocketed the cash with a poised hand next to his gun.

He understood the rules of the ghetto and the viciousness of it; cutthroats. A deal with a shyster could be as deadly as be- friending a cobra.

Tone continuously peeped over a shoulder while quickstep- ping to Tang's, a local takeout joint. After ordering a pack of Newport and six buffalo wings, he headed across the street to "The Lounge," a dive recognized for its drug trafficking: more so, than its winery. He returned to Tang's small, empty, ante- room toting a brown bag containing two forty-ounce bottles of beer. In his jeans-pocket, six nickel-vials of crack. "Tang! Yo, Tang!" he hollered. "You got my grub yet?"

The Korean hustled to the plexiglass with a finger pursed against thin lips. "Shh…" he cautioned, "your foo' no ready. Fi' minute still."

"Why y'all so fuckin' slow?" Tone replied sarcastically.

He whirled from the window and flopped onto a small wooden bench. He took a long swig of beer while eyeballing two teenage girls enter the store.

One was brown-skinned and chubby while the other glowed a deep chocolate and had jet black hair, cut short and waved. She wore brown lipstick to match her big brown eyes, and her body was full and ripe for what Tone had in mind.

Tone stared open-mouthed while she read the menu. He put away the beer and stepped to the counter. "How you doing?" he asked, trying to fight back his shyness where girls were concerned.

Their eyes locked. "Fine," she answered softly, then continued surveying the menu.

"Girl, I'll be outside," the chubby friend stated. "You from aroun' here?" Tone asked.

"Yeah."

"Then why I ain't never seen you?"

"Cause, you the one that ain't from around here," she replied matter of fact.

"What's your name?"

"Stacey."

"Stacey, anybody ever tell you how fine you look?"

She giggled a conceited "yes" then added a "sike,"

"…and a cute," Tone added.

"Thank you"

"Where your man at?" Tone asked.

"A man," she said defensively. "I'm too young for a man."

"Yeah right," he trilled. "How old are you?"

"Sixteen"

"You playin'?"

"I ain't playing," she assured him, drumming four slim fingers on the counter.

"Well, dig this, sweet sixteen…how 'bout us gettin' together sometime?"

"I can't do that."

"Why?"

"I don't even know you."

"I'm Tone."

"Six shickon wing!" Tang hollered, shoving Tone's bag through the window.

"Stacey, come 'ere, girl," her plump friend called from the door. "Ain't that Marcus ass getting locked the hell up?"

Stacey scrambled to the door just as handcuffs were being placed on her brother.

Tone watched Stacey, from Tang's doorway, sprint to her brother's side. He took one look at the stolen B.M.W. he'd sold, and already knew the charges. Not until the police were gone and the crowd dispersed, did he exit the store.

"Damn. That was your brother?" Tone asked Stacey.

"Yeah. That's his sorry ass."

"You all right?"

"Yeah. I'm cool."

Tone felt bad for her. Her tears indicated the closeness she and her brother shared. As an only child, Tone had little inkling of her despair and little patience for comforting. "Look, I gotta go right now. Can I call you?"

She breathed deeply. "I don't know about all that."

"Why not?"

"How about you give me your number and I'll call you?"

"Why you playin' me like this?" He stepped closer to her and reached for her hand. It felt velvety. "You ain't gonna call me, are you?"

"Yes, I will."

Tone had no idea if she'd call or not. He only knew that he wanted this girl. He borrowed a pen from The Lounge and scribbled his number on a chunk of paper bag.

Chapter Four

A month has passed since the Montross killings and, once again, Ryan rewound the surveillance tape he'd received from Officer Murrell. The coroner had placed the deaths between two and seven a.m., supporting his theory that the murderer was one of Candy's customers. Ryan had already questioned many people appearing on the videotape and had come away empty. The ones that have been identified but haven't been questioned were being sought. After thirty minutes of studying faces, he clicked off the V.C.R. and sat back sipping iced soda from a tall glass Deitra had won at a carnival two summers ago. He swished the drink around in his mouth until the tingling bubbles subsided and shifted his thoughts to Jane Doe.

It's been a week since he'd visited Jane Doe. A phone call to Doctor Hughes has become easier. Besides, he reasoned, the doctor had assured him she'd call with news of any change of the woman's condition. Outside, the sun beamed invisible streams of fire down on Philadelphia. Even the subtlest of breezes wanted no parts of the wicked heatwave blanketing the East Coast.

Ryan rushed from the house and into the Plymouth. While he waited for the air-conditioner to crank out cool air around him, he unpocketed his cellphone and dialed his in-law's number.

His five-year-old answered.

"Hey, Pumpkin." he mused.

"Daddy!" the child caroled, loud enough to force him to pull the phone from his ear.

"Alright…Calm down, Baby. How are you?"

"Fine."

"Just fine?"

"Yes."

"How's Grandma and Grandpop?"

"Fine."

Ryan smiled at the sound of cartoons filtering from the background. He wondered if Brenda's eyes were dancing lively in their sockets like they did when he'd watch cartoons with her. "Where's your, mommy, Brenda?"

"Upstairs."

"Can you tell her to pick up the phone for me?"

"O.K. Hold on, Daddy."

"I will."

Over two minutes past before Ryan heard Brenda giggle on the line. "Hello?" he asked wonderingly.

"Huh?"

"Brenda?"

"Yes."

"I thought you were going to get your mommy for me?"

"O.K. Hold on, Daddy…Mommy!" the child

screamed, pulling a smile from Ryan.

Seconds later, Deitra's husky voice was on the line.

"It's me, Dee." Ryan said.

"I know it's you."

"I'm just checking to see if everything is fine."

"Mm-hmm. Is that all?"

Ryan sunk deeper into the Plymouth's seat. He felt like a school kid busted whizzing paper balls at the teacher's back. He took a deep breath before confessing. "Well, that's not the main reason."

"Then what is?"

He paused for what he thought was too long. "O.K. So, I'm sweating you a bit. Can you blame me for wanting you home? I miss you. And I know the kids are starting to drive your parents nuts.

"Ryan, I told you I'd think about it." Her tone was easy. He sensed that she, too, was tired of the separation.

"Have I been that bad a husband?"

"No, Ryan, you haven't. You also haven't shown me that you can slow down from working. Am I supposed to just believe you, now?"

"Yes. You are Dee, You're my wife."

For several seconds, their words were thoughts.

Ryan broke the silence. "Look, I know my work interfered with our lives, but I'm promising you…right now. It'll never happen again." He listened to her light sniffing and wanted so much to comfort her. To carry each tear that drips from her eyes on his shoulder.

"Oh, Ryan," she sniffed, "I want to believe you so badly."

"You can, Dee. All you have to do, Sweetheart, is come home."

Ryan hung up the phone, slightly optimistic. He felt he'd finally gotten through to Deitra, or was it, she'd finally gotten through to him? Nevertheless, he glowed with joy. He felt more energized than he'd felt in months. And with confidence, he sang his and Deitra's favorite song, "Still in Love," by Luther Vandross, as he whipped through traffic toward the precinct.

The precinct was packed, as it usually is during the midday peak of court hearings and bookings. Ryan felt as fresh as if he'd had a full night's rest. He'd spent most of the night questioning vagabonds, who roamed Saigon's halls during the wee hours. He'd hoped to run across anyone who'd heard a whisper of relevance pertaining to the Montross' murders. Unfortunately, he didn't.

"Page!" a voice boomed.

Ryan recognized it as Plummer's.

I'd like a word with you in my office, Detective.

Ryan shuffled into the office and closed the door. "What's up, Captain?"

"How's your caseload, Ryan?"

"It's coining along."

"Good. How about the Montross case? You getting anywhere with that one?"

"It's been tough. Discouraging."

"You know that kind of attitude doesn't solve cases, right?"

"I don't know. It seems whoever's responsible just vanished. Came and went. No prints. No news. No eye-witnesses - well, there is one witness, but she's comatose."

"I know it's frustrating, Ryan, but I'm sure you'll come up with something."

"Thanks for the vote of confidence."

"Yeah-yeah," Plummer dismissed. "In the meantime, do you remember me mentioning the Mayor wanting to build a mini police station?"

"Yeah. I remember."

"Well, that's what I want to talk to you about. A public consensus needs to be taken. Although I doubt there'll be much objection to build it, we need to maintain good public relations." Plummer pulled a white handkerchief from his back pants pocket and blew his nose.

"So why talk to me? Sounds like you have a plan."

Plummer came from behind his desk and sat on its edge. His expression solemn. A politician's stare. "Ryan, I need you to represent this district."

It was Ryan's turn to stare. "What do you mean represent?" he asked.

"You know…talk to the community. Answer questions. That sort of thing."

"You mean the blacks in the community."

"Well, yeah. Is there something wrong with that. It is predominately minority."

"Come on, Captain. You know my plate is full already."

"I know. But with this, all you'll have to do is make an appearance, say a few words, then escape."

Ryan thought for a moment. "I don't know. Maybe."

"Ryan, this could be your chance to bump elbows

with the brass. If I were you, I 'd take it. It could flavor your resume; if you know what I mean it

Ryan knew exactly what he meant. In other words, if he refused, the higher-ups would not forget come promotions. "Can I get back to you?"

"Certainly. Take your time. We have at least two weeks, but, for now, concentrate on solving this dang Montross thing."

The parking lots surrounding the Corestate Spectrum were packed with beaded deadheads draped in tie-dyes and signs begging for the exact thing - tickets to witness the legendary Grateful Dead in concert. For three full days, 150,000 hardcore fans will camp in trucks, cars, and tents around the stadium.

For many deadheads, the tailgate parties make traveling thousands of miles well worth it. For others, the business opportunities were endless.

Hustling came instinctively for Daewoo, as it came to other Players, who chased a dollar during the concerts. It was days like today the "Slum Game" proved gold. Fake mushrooms, cocaine, marijuana, acid, opium, and personalities are all the tools necessary to play the game, and Daewoo had done right to stock up on his. In two hours of work, Daewoo sold four-hundred-sixty dollars' worth of slum and flirted with the idea of quitting. Twenty minutes later, he found himself on the subway train separating get-high money from what he assumed would eventually become get-high money after the first stash was gone.

Although Webster Street appeared crude and impoverished, a wealth of cash flowed through it. Each day, more money exchanged hands on the small, deserted street than in all the local grocery stores combined, creating a haven for drug dealers. It also held one of the ghetto's most frequented smokehouses.

After copping ten nicks and renting a room, Daewoo anxiously enjoyed his first hit of the day. Two hours passed before his paranoia surfaced and beads of sweat streamed from his bald-head. Breathing had also become a task, and frequently he'd pace the tiny, windowless room gasping for air.

Daewoo left the smokehouse with blurry vision and his paranoia pushed to the brink. He'd not been outside a full minute before a police car routinely turned onto Webster Street. Delusional, he took off running in the opposite direction, not bothering to glance back until he was six blocks away, behind a schoolyard wall, at 6th & Banbridge.

He breathed deeply to calm himself, afraid of the rumors he'd heard about cocaine bursting the hearts of people during high anxiety attacks. "I swear I'm leavin' this shit alone," he mumbled before quickly leaving the schoolyard in search of a bar.

The pub was sparsely furnished. Three antique ceiling fans hung sheathed by a thick cloud of cigar smoke. A huge circular bar dominated the pub's center and several tabled booths, with punished orange leather chairs, lined the farthest wall where three Italian men tossed darts at a board fifteen feet away.

Daewoo adjusted his eyes to the lighting and quickly noticed he was the only black in the place. He fought back the urge to leave, took a seat at the bar and ordered a double rum and coke. He felt several eyes behind him staring, pinching his back like tiny needles. If not for needing a drink in the worst way, he'd have left the place. Instead, he kept his eyes to himself, gulped down the first drink and ordered another.

After a third drink had loosened him up and eliminated his skits, he pulled a crumpled Newport from its pack and eyeballed the dart game. He even felt well enough to toy with the idea of slumming someone in the bar then thought better of it when his palm rested on the roll of cash in his pocket.

"Something else, Buddy?" the bartender asked.

Daewoo peered down at his empty glass. "Yeah, a beer."

"What kind?"

"Old English."

"Don't serve it."

"How 'bout Colt 45?"

"How 'bout Budweiser?"

"That's cool. Give me that."

When the bartender returned, Daewoo scooped up his beer and dawdled over to the dart game. He had little interest in darts, but it was the only action that seemed to be going on.

"You play?"

Daewoo turned to survey a white-haired man around fifty or so. "Nope," he answered.

"I seen you around South Street, ain't I?" the man asked, tipping his head for a better look.

"Probably."

The man stepped forward and whispered, "You know it's no secret what you guys do down there."

"And what's that?" Daewoo asked, feeling he'd already stayed to long.

"Selling that beat shit."

Daewoo shook his head no. "You must got me mixed up with somebody."

"If you say so. I just hope you ain't come in here for that."

Daewoo glanced around first for witnesses to their conversation then for others he assumed would want him thrown out. He swigged his beer to mask his discontent. "I just came in for a drink," he countered.

"Well, I thought I'd let you know before you get yourself into trouble."

Daewoo couldn't help but admire the man's honesty. It was obvious the man was no mark.

"What's your name, Kid?"

"Daewoo."

"Please to meet you, Daewoo. I'm Frank Russo. You might 'a heard 'a me before."

"I don't think so." Daewoo twisted his face in thought.

Frank twirled a thin straw around in his drink. "Hell, I don't know if that's good or bad," he remarked. "Tell me something, Daewoo…You make any doe selling that beat shit?"

Daewoo looked at the man dumbfounded. "Selling what?"

Frank let loose a booming laugh that drew nearly

every eye in their direction. "Selling what?" he mused. "You gotta be fucking kidding me?" Frank lifted a halting hand in surrender. "O.K., I get the point. How about another beer?"

For an hour, Daewoo listened to Frank, while they drank, go on and on about scams, politicians, and crooked cops. He hadn't intended on getting drunk, but, with Frank, drinking seemed the thing to do.

Daewoo had heard that Italians loved to drink, but the number of margaritas Frank had tossed into his thin 5'10 frame was ridiculous.

Behind Frank's small, gold spectacles, were hollow, blue eyes that continuously darted from side to side every few seconds. Two huge ears protruded from the man's head and although Daewoo found a humorous quality in Frank's appearance, looking at the man did not make you laugh. It piqued curiosity.

Frank stubbed his eighth cigarette since they've met. He turned a cold stare to Daewoo. "You like money?" he asked.

Daewoo smiled. "Do I? More than pussy."

"That's good. You think you can make money?"

"I get mine."

"Fuck just getting yours!" Frank bursted. "I'm talking about getting rich beyond your fucking wildest dreams." Frank's outburst surprised Daewoo. He wondered if the margaritas had finally caught up to the man then realized the conviction in Frank's words and the sincerity on the man's face. "Daewoo, are you tough?"

"What do you mean tough?"

"You know… tough. Able to handle yourself."

"I'm tough enough."

"Never mind," Frank dismissed, "you're probably not the guy I'm looking for."

Daewoo looked at Frank offended. "Man, what the hell you talkin' 'bout? Ain't a motherfucker in "here" can kick my ass."

"That's good, Daewoo, because I need workers."

"Doin' what?"

"That's not important right now. How about jotting your number down and I'll get back to you?"

Daewoo bummed a pen from the bartender and scribbled Trina mother's phone number on a napkin.

"I hope you are who you say," Frank warned. "I'ma have my people check you out. If everything checks out, I'll give a you call tomorrow around six."

Daewoo exited the bar drunk and excited at the possibility of a window of opportunity being opened. He looked up at the neon sign hanging over the pub's doorway. **"Little Italy"** it read.

Near 4 p.m., the buttery aroma of fresh-baked rolls filled the small, two-story home. The tiny living room was decorated with fake Victorian furniture, and on the sofa, Tone roused from his sleep because of the tickling scent awakening his monstrous hunger pangs. He turned toward the wall clock. "Damn," he muttered, realizing he'd slept over eleven hours. He dragged his thin, stilly-clothed frame into the kitchen and began peeping into four simmering pots on the stove. He wondered why his mother hadn't awaken' him and sent him upstairs to bed. His mulling ceased at the sound of the front door slamming shut. Quickly he tried to recover the pots before his mother reached the kitchen, but, before he could, she was grimacing.

"Boy, get your narrow ass out my pots!" she hollered.

Tone smiled boyishly and stepped away from the stove. "I was just lookin'."

"You could've just asked too. I know you ain't washed your nasty ass hands."

Tone loved his mother and her old-fashion way of thinking. To him, she was more like a friend than a mother, giving him free reign to go and come as he chose mostly. He pecked her on the cheek. "Good mornin'," he offered.

"Good morning? It's more like evening, but good morning to you too…if this is your kind of morning." She smoothed back her shiny black hair with hands too small for her lengthy arms. With a thick, tan rubber band, she tied her small ponytail.

Still, at thirty-seven, her youth beamed. Her tan oval face was small, and she peered at Tone with large, criticizing eyes. "You just like your damn father. He used to waltz his yellow ass in here all times 'a night too."

Tone frowned. "Mom, I don't know why you frontin'. You know you ain't care what time Dad came home."

"Oh, I cared. I just never said anything. Plus, you ain't your daddy, so bring your ass in here at a decent hour. You hear me?"

Tone was in no mood to argue. She'd given him the same speech a dozen times before. He knew it made her feel good to have something to tell her girlfriends. Something about setting rules and disciplining teenagers.

With a small, "Mm-hmm," he retreated back to the sofa. No sooner he sat down, he heard his mother holler, "And get that shit outta my living room, too!"

"Alright. Damn," he barked, but just loud enough for her not to hear. He snatched up his keys and cigarettes from the coffee table, his Fila sneakers from the floor then headed upstairs.

While Tone showered and dressed, his thoughts centered around Candy and Daewoo. Maybe he should've slumped Daewoo, he thought, something he wondered about ever since the two had parted ways. There was always the change of Daewoo snitching. He pulled the sleeveless, silk, maroon T-shirt over his head and decided to pay Daewoo a visit soon - not to kill him, but to remind Daewoo of the stakes.

After wolfing down a huge plate of meatloaf, rice-a-roni, string-beans, and buttered rolls, Tone lounged on the sofa dragging lovely from a Newport. Lazily, he watched his mother fuss after two baby ferns hanging from a ceiling hook. "Morn, that grub was mean," he complimented.

She turned from her plants and smiled appreciatively. "Why thank you. I'd never know you appreciate my food the way you run them damn streets."

"Now you know. Plus, I'ma 'bout to slow down."

"Tony, boy," she said with a smirk, preferring Tony over Tone, which she'd called his father, "you always talking that mess. I know one thing…I ain't taking care of no babies, so you better not try bringing any in here."

"Mom, you trippin'. Ain't nobody thinkin' 'bout bringin' no kids in your house."

"Don't I know it," she countered before turning back to her plants.

Their conversation pushed Tone's thoughts to Stacey, the girl he'd met at Tang's. Why hadn't she called him? He knew a relationship with the girl was probably doomed; after all, he did sell her brother a stolen car minutes after a police chase. But regardless of that, he wanted to see her again…and again.

At 7:15, the evening air hung heavy and dry. The night sky had not yet descended on the South Philadelphia ghetto, and the neighborhood children hurried to cram in their last games of double-Dutch, penny pitching, and tops before their mothers called to save them from the madness of night-time. Tone had left the house with his mother's sermon erased from his mind. He loved her for her efforts but scoffed at her for not knowing him at all. He passed the ghetto children at play as he strolled toward 13th Street project. In a way, he envied the children's innocence as they playfully enjoyed life. For him, life seems a task. And because his game could easily end in death, living seemed anything but simple, especially since his father's death three years ago. His father had done as he pleased during life. He was a notorious gambler, numbers runner, and full-time alcoholic. He'd made it a point to spoil Tone rotten, and because of it, Tone looked to him with enormous pride. When he'd died, any hopes of doing good had died in Tone as well.

Nine men stood semi-circled at the corner of 13th & Catherine Streets. Each man paid close attention to the tenth man in a squat.

"Eight, dammit!" the shooter roared, then scrambled to collect three stacks of bills at his feet. Tone saw the crap game and smiled.

The shooter was Jamaica, a known dealer, who Tone had gambled before. He'd been impressed with Jamaica's shot. As he neared the game, he pulled four crumpled one-dollar bills farm his pocket and smoothed them out as he searched each player's face. He settled on a man he'd never seen before. A slim, bearded man with telling eyes and an oversized Armani sweatsuit. Jamaica's point was 6, not a difficult point to make, but side-bettors still challenged the odds. Tone bet his four bucks with the shooter.

Jamaica's first roll was 3, his second a 10, and his third roll a 9. On the fourth roll, with the flair of a magician, Jamaica plucked up the dice, blew on them, then rattled them hard before tossing them against the wall. Sure enough, two 3's showed.

"Yes," Tone whispered. He collected his winnings and waited on the next point.

In craps, 9 only shows two ways: five-four or six-three. All around, odds were being laid. Tone received 2 to 1 odds on his eight dollars. He dropped the money to the ground and step- ped on it. 4 was the first roll. 3 the second. On the third roll the dice spun for close to ten seconds then stopped to show five-deuce. Tone lost.

Reluctantly, Tone lifted his foot from the money and con- templated sticking up the game. So caught up in his anger, he hadn't noticed Jamaica's new point until the man he'd been betting asked, "Still betting or what?"

Not wanting to let the man know he was broke, Tone said, "Yeah," unworried about the consequences of ass-betting the guy. If push came to shove, Tone thought, he'd shoot the chump, and just in case the man expected to see the cash, Tone faded to the opposite side of the crowd, pretending to place another bet.

The point again was 9. The first roll 3, the second eight, and the third a 6. On the fourth roll, one die showed 5 while the other spun on its edge until the fader interrupted it with a foot.

"These mines," the fader called, fearing the die would stop on 4.

"Man, let the motherfucker roll!" a better barked. Jamaica, unflinched, again plucked up the dice, but instead of shaking them, he clicked them four times in one hand before swiftly tossing them against the wall. "Nine!" he yelled, and on command, the dice bucked a few times and stopped showing six-three.

"Oh, yeah," Tone said as he made himself available to collect his bet.

After an hour, Tone had raised his winnings to fifty-two dollars and decided to quit.

The daylight sky was quickly fading and as the summer temperature eased to tolerable, more neighborhood residents ventured outdoors. Tone stood on Tang's stoop sipping pineapple soda from a bottle and watching a crowd flock toward a fight between two children. Instinctively, he wandered over as well. When he reached the crowd, he smiled at the sight of Stacey separating two small boys.

"Go home, Boy!" she yelled at the smaller child,

pouting a protest. "I don't care!" she argued, shoving the boy toward 1241 building.

Even before she turned around, Tone was there sporting an immobile look.

"Hey, Tone," she greeted expressionless.

"What's up?" Tone replied, noting she looked even finer than he remembered. "Who was shorty?"

"My nephew." Tone grinned. "What's so funny?"

"Nothin' really. It just seem like whenever I run into you, somebody in your family in trouble."

"This ain't the half of it," she stated.

The crowd had dispersed and now the two of them stood alone.

"Why you ain't call me?" Tone asked, hoping his tone hid his disappointment.

"I did call."

"Girl, stop lyin'."

"I did," she insisted.

"Well, my peeps ain't say nothin' 'bout it."

Stacey shrugged. "I guess that's something you gotta work out, huh?"

"Why you just ain't call back?"

Stacey sucked her pearly white teeth and rolled her eyes. "Tone, you was running around with your homies. I don't even know why you standing here frontin'."

"Nah, not me," he lied as they started to walk.

Ridgeway stretched a full city block. It included a swimming pool, two basketball courts, and a dark, secluded hideaway where neighborhood teens hid to get high.

Tone remembered his days in the playground as he

peeled away the cigar's cellophane wrapping, meticulously sliced down its middle, and dumped its tobacco in the grass. "I'ma show you how to make a blunt," he boasted, his words pulling a tiny smile from Stacey. He opened the small package of marijuana and sniffed it. "Booyah!" he yelled. "Smell like we got some Buddha weed here."

After tearing the cigar wrapping in two, he pasted them together with saliva then filled them with weed. When the blunt was rolled, he set it aside to dry. "What's up with your brother?" he asked. "He get out yet?"

"Nope. That fool still locked up. He had a bench warrant for drugs."

"Damn. That shit's wac. I feel for him."

"He'll be all right. He say he didn't steal that car."

"Do you believe him?" Tone asked. He picked up the blunt and lit it.

"Yeah. I believe him. He ain't got no reason to lie to me. I ain't the judge. He probably got it from one of his sorry ass friends."

"Yeah. That's usually how it go down," Tone agreed. "I don't think he did it either."

"How do you know? You don't even know him."

"But I know *you* and trust your judgement." Stacey blushed.

Her smile was inviting, and for a moment, Tone felt attached to her. He passed her the blunt then stood. "You know what we need?" he asked.

Stacey choked back the smoke threatening to escape her lungs. "No, what?"

"Some music."

"That would be nice," she agreed.

With Stacey, Tone felt at ease. An easiness he'd not felt in a long time. Trusting people has always been a shortcoming for him, but he trusted Stacey and felt as if everything wonderful extended from her. He felt good and, without shame, began rapping. Slowly at first, then, with passion. He could tell from her reaction that she was impressed. Her head rocked back and forth with his every word, and her smile was as genuine of a smile he's ever seen. It was here he knew he'd win her heart.

Another day of sweltering heat engulfed the east coast. For many adults, adapting to its discomfort was impossible, and yet, hordes of children soaked themselves in the streets' fire-hydrants seemingly unfazed by the heat. Ryan slammed on the car's brakes to avoid a teenage boy dashing across the street, shouldering a bucket of water. "Get out the street!" Ryan hollered from his car window. He immediately regretted saying anything at all as the teenager glared menacingly then tossed the bucket of water on the car's wind- shield. Most of the water landed flush, but some spilled into the car. "Goddammit!" Ryan yelled. He wanted to chase the youth down but was too anxious to get to Pennsylvania Hospital. Ten minutes ago, Doctor Hughes had phoned to report that Jane Doe had regained consciousness. Finally, Ryan thought, a real break in the case has come. The short walk from the visitors' parking lot had bereaved Ryan of energy, and the hospital's cool air was replenishing as if a cold blanket had been placed around his body. He waited for the receptionist to page the doctor.

"She'll be down in a moment, Detective," said the receptionist. "If you'd like to wait in the cafeteria, I'll inform Doctor Hughes where you are," she offered.

"I'll do that. Thank you." Ryan had just bitten into his second cheeseburger when Doctor Hughes entered the cafeteria and began scanning faces. She carried a yellow manila envelope tucked under one am.

Ryan half-stood and grabbed an arm. She looked younger than Ryan remembered, and her wet honey-colored hair was pulled back in a soft chignon. Her gait was sort of a bounce across the cafeteria, and Ryan sensed she kept herself in good physical condition.

"Hello, Detective," she greeted in a deep feminine baritone.

"How you doing, Doctor?" He waved to the seat across from his. "Have a seat."

"I'm sorry, Detective, but I only have a few minutes."

"Well, in that case, how's the patient?"

She breathed deeply, then pulled several documents from the envelope and scanned their text. She looked up at Ryan, who nervously drummed three fingers on the table. "Well, to be honest, she's still in profoundly serious condition, not critical but serious, nonetheless. We are, however, optimistic about her recovery. She's regained conscious, for now, but with a head injury as serious as hers, she could very easily slip back into a comatose state."

Ryan scooted his head forward. "Doc, I don't want to sound insensitive, but what about her memory? Has she said anything about what happened?"

"I'm afraid not. Which is quite normal."

Ryan rewrapped his burger then balled it up, his appetite diminished. "Normal, huh?"

"Certainly. It's just one of many complications."

"What are the other kinds?"

"There could be a number of things." She extended a slim finger with each thing she counted off. "Speech impairment, clogging of the brain's blood vessels, memory loss, hemorrhaging…"

"O.K. O.K., I get the picture."

"Detective, it's still too early to give a definite analysis. I only did as you asked and notified you of her status change."

"You're right, Doc. I appreciate it."

"No problem. But tell me something…" she questioned.

"What's that?"

"Why haven't anyone been able to identify her?"

"I wish I knew. I ran her prints, contacted missing persons, but nothing came up."

"She's a mystery to us as well. When do you think I'll be able to speak with her?"

She shuffled through the papers again then slid them back into the envelope. "In about four hours. Maybe." She emphasized maybe. "If she's not in pain and willing to talk, I may be able to allow a few minutes, tops."

Ryan returned to a busy precinct high spirited. Things were finally starting to look promising at work as well as at home.

Over the weekend, he and Deitra had, at last, resolved most of their differences. It was now up to him to manage his priorities between work and family. He wasn't surprised Deitra wanted to wait until the Montross case was settled before returning home. She knew him well enough to realize his emotional involvement in the case and agreed to a vacation when it ended.

Ryan found it obvious Deitra missed being home equally as much as he missed her being there. At times, he'd returned home to find the previous night's mess cleaned, plants watered, and items of clothes missing from their closet as well as the children's. The sooner the case was over, he thought, the sooner he could get on with his life.

Ryan pushed away the file he'd been working on and headed towards Plummer's office. The open door indicated that the captain was in a good mood. "Captain," Ryan said, tapping the door twice.

Plummer's head rose from the pile of papers on his desk.

He sat back in his chair. "Ryan, come in. What can I do for you?"

"I thought you'd like to know that Jane Doe's out of her coma."

"That's wonderful. Maybe she's what you need to jump-start this case, huh? She seems to be the link, right?"

Yes, she does.

"Good. I'll be glad when it's over," Plummer said. He came from behind his desk. "By the way, Ryan, have you prepared a speech for the town-house meeting next week?"

Ryan's eyes narrowed as he considered the question.

"Next week?" he answered.

Plummer tossed his hands up unbelievingly. "Oh, Christ, Ryan, don't tell me you forgot!"

"No. I didn't forget."

"I hope not," Plummer added. "You know, Ryan, this could be very important for your career in the department."

"I know, Captain. It's just that there's been a lot on my mind lately."

Plummer stepped forward and placed a pudgy hand on Ryan's shoulder. "Look, Son, I can understand why you're anxious to clear this case - it's priority - no doubt about it. But you gotta remember, Ryan, that there's more going on in your life besides this case."

"You don't have to remind me of that."

"I'm sure I don't. But I've seen a lot of good men drag themselves down over the years. I'd hate to think your heading down that path."

Ryan shook his head in acknowledgement. "So, you had lunch yet?" Plummer asked.

"Yeah, I picked up a couple burgers over at Penn."

"Well, I guess there's no need inviting you then. Is there anything else you need?"

"No."

"Good. Now, if you'll excuse me, I have a pile of reports to finish."

For the next hour, Ryan mulled over numerous mugshots and video surveillance tapes he intended to present to Jane Doe.

When the time arrived for Ryan to return to the hospital, he found his palms moist and his heartbeat increasing. He knew the feeling well. It was the exact way he'd felt in high school just before a big game.

Pennsylvania Hospital's I.C.U. was located on the third floor. As Ryan passed the nurses station, the head nurse called after him. "Excuse me. Detective Page?"

"Yes," Ryan answered.

"Hi. I'm Nurse Blanchard. Doctor Hughes asked me to have you wait for her before you visit with Ms. Doe."

"How long do you think that'll be?"

"She'll be here shortly," she said simply. "You can wait over there." She pointed to a row of six chairs just outside of Jane Doe's room.

Ryan took a seat and pulled a short list of questions from his pocket. Usually, he need not bother jotting down questions, but, because of Jane Doe's coma, there were questions he wasn't able to ask.

Five minutes passed before Doctor Hughes stepped from the elevator. "Detective," she greeted. "I see you're exceedingly punctual."

"Not always," he admitted. Ryan stood and smiled down at the doctor.

"That makes two of us. Shall we?"

Ryan hadn't visited Jane Doe in three weeks, but this woman couldn't be the same one he'd visited then. This woman looked near death - frail, a skeleton - as if, the days have sucked every ounce of nourishment from her body. He approached the bed as if her condition was contagious. He couldn't explain the eerie feeling he felt when, with a sickly hand, she stretched the starched bedspread to her chin, in an attempt to cover herself, as if he was the cause of her being there. He gathered himself and pasted a false smile to his face. "Miss Gordon, how are you?" Dr. Hughes asked.

Ryan's head jerked toward the doctor when she addressed the woman by name.

"This is Detective Page of the Philadelphia Police Department," she continued. "He'd like to talk to you about what happened. O.K.?"

The woman's eyes, once wide and bulged, were now small slits of sorrow as they turned curiously to Ryan.

On cue, Ryan stepped forward, only now, his false smile was true compassion. He cleared his throat before speaking. "Miss Gordon, what's your full name?"

She slid a dry tongue across parched lips and mumbled, "Malissa Gordon."

Ryan barely heard her. He took a seat at her bedside and leaned closer. "Did you say Malissa Gordon?" he asked.

Malissa nodded.

"Who shot you, Malissa?"

She swallowed hard and closed her eyes tightly. When she reopened them, a single tear streamed down her bony cheek. "I…I don't know," she croaked.

"Did you see who shot you?" he asked. Again, she nodded.

"But you didn't know him?"

"No."

"If you saw him again, would you recognize him?"

"Yes," she whispered.

Ryan felt a jolt of relief surge through him.

Dr. Hughes raised Malissa's wrist and checked her pulse. "Are you all right?" she asked.

Malissa fingered the head bandage. "My head hurt," she whined softly.

"I'll get something for you," the doctor said. On her way out, she whispered to Ryan not to overdo it.

"I won't," he replied.

When the doctor was gone, he turned back to Malissa. "Miss Gordon," he said with compassion, "I know you're going through a tough ordeal, but it's especially important that you put whoever did this to you behind bars. We believe that the same guy who shot you also murdered an elderly couple across the street from where you were found."

Her tears had become constant.

Ryan feared she'd drain her frail body of fluids. He looked directly into her eyes. "Is there anything you can tell me about this guy?" he asked.

She turned watery eyes to the ceiling and stared. In a weak voice, close to a mumble, she uttered, "There was two of 'em."

Doctor Hughes returned to the room. "I'm sorry, Detective, I'm going to have to ask you to do this another time."

Ryan didn't want to seem pushy. "Sure. Is tomorrow O.K.?"

"We'll see," said the doctor as she turned to Malissa.

The following morning, the small alarm clock's clanging snatched Ryan from his sleep. Slowly, without looking, he slapped at the noise until the buzzing ceased. After showering, a pop-tart breakfast with coffee, he was wide awake and anxious to question Malissa Gordon. He'd hoped to show her a few mug- shots of possible suspects yesterday, but, while visiting the woman, he realized the severity of her condition. He hoped today he'd fare better.

Until morning passed and the hospital's visiting hours arrived, Ryan trudged through several new cases he'd been assigned. At 1:10 p.m., he pulled into the hospital's parking area. He would have arrived sooner if not for the quick stop at a Kentucky Fried Chicken drive-through, but the effects of his mini-breakfast bad taken its toll.

While he finished his meal, he tangled with his guilt about questioning Malissa. He wondered if his real concern was himself and not her - or, in that case, Candy or Paul Montross. He wiped the chicken grease from his fingers and grabbed the photo-filled envelope from the passenger seat. At the hospital entrance, a small Korean woman, hidden beneath a large straw sombrero, stood peddling bouquets.

"How much?" Ryan asked.

"Fl' dollar."

"I'll take one."

Ryan knocked before entering Malissa's room; The drapes were drawn shut, forbidding any daylight from disturbing the woman lain on her back, resembling death. He placed the bouquet in an empty vase atop a small table near the bed and stared down at the woman.

Her eyes were closed, and her chapped lips parted slightly.

In each nostril, a long, thin, clear tube protruded.

Ryan traced them to a respiratory system on the other side of the bed. Her chest rose with each tiny breath she took.

He felt sorry for her and angry at himself for having to

disturb her rest. He called her name softly. "Miss Gordon." He leaned closer. "Miss Gordon, can you hear me?" He pulled back a bit when her eyes fluttered open.

She twisted her head to face him. "How are you?" he asked.

Mustering strength, she cleared her throat. "O.K. I guess."

"That's good. I'm sure they're doing everything here to get you well."

Their eyes locked in several seconds. In that time, Ryan felt he knew her and all the cliches of every poor, black girl scrambling through the ghetto streets on drugs. He pulled himself from her stare. "Uhm…listen," he stammered. "I brought by a few photos I'd like you to look over." He paused a few seconds, anticipating a reaction. When none came, he continued. "I know you may not feel up to talking right now, but if you recognize any of these men as one of the two people we spoke about yesterday, all you have to do is nod. O.K.?"

Malissa nodded.

The photos were mugshots of black men with records of assaults, between the ages of 18 - 40, each living in or around Saigon. Because Malissa had recognized both suspects from 13th Street, Ryan had concentrated there. He'd hoped she'd identify at least one of the suspects, but after placing photos in front of her face for an hour, his hope deteriorated. He left his home number with Malissa, just in case, and left the hospital optimistic. Perhaps, he thought, he needed to retrace his steps. Perhaps he'd missed something or someone.

He sat in the Plymouth until the air conditioning enveloped him. He'd spent most of the morning clearing paperwork from his desk, and with no intention of retackling the task, he gently pulled from the parking lot into traffic.

Chapter Five

Daylight forced Daewoo to open still-tired eyes as he shivered and pulled the thin cotton sheet tighter around his naked body. He lay still, remembering the night's drinking. When the cobwebs cleared, he headed, dry-mouthed and naked, into the kitchen. It's been nearly a month since Daewoo had received the job delivering drugs to wealthy clients of Frank Russo's spread across the tri-state. The job was simple, as were the risks. What excited Daewoo most was the thirteen hundred a week salary; although he did miss hustling, something Frank stressed would compromise Daewoo's loyalty to the job.

Without needing to roam the streets as much for cash, Daewoo found himself hibernating at home and using far less cocaine. For him, the change was refreshing, especially since Trina had begun spending more time at home, making the transformation all more worthwhile. Daewoo had never bothered to look into the living room.

If he'd have, he'd have noticed Trina and his four-year-old, Divon, staring as he guzzled water from a plastic gallon jug he'd pulled from the fridge.

"Daewoo!" Trina yelled.

Daewoo jerked his head around, tipping a stream of cold water down his bare chest. "Shit!" he screamed. He glared at the two of them laughing. "Damn, Girl, what the hell? You scared the shit outta me."

"Look at you," she scolded. "You need to put some drawers on your ashy ass."

"I ain't even know you was here."

"Is this how you walk around when I'm not?"

"Sometimes," he answered, retreating to the bedroom.

Daewoo returned wearing faded blue jeans and flopped on the sofa next to Trina and Divon. "Hey, Little Man," he said extremely jovial. He pulled the child onto his lap.

"You do know what time it is, don't you?" Trina asked.

"Yeah, I know." He wrapped his shoulders with part of the bedspread Trina sat under. "Well?"

"Well, what?"

"Well, you just sitting there. You need to get dressed and take your ass to work."

"Girl, I know. Please don't start trippin'."

"Don't worry, I not even gonna trip." Her tone was dismissive, but her eyes were pleading. "It's just that you been doing so good."

"I know, Baby. You ain't gotta worry 'bout me goin' that route again."

"Mm-hm," she hummed with twisted lips. "It's always something with you, Daewoo."

He knew she had a legitimate beef and pointed to the

T.V. "What's this?" he asked, changing the subject. He could feel her stare turn from him to the television.

"Barney," she simply said.

"Who the hell is Barney?"

"It's for the kids, Dum Dum." She playfully smacked his arm.

"Yeah, well, I see it's time for me to raise up outta here. You gonna be here when I get home?"

"No."

"Why not?"

She sucked her teeth. "'Cause, you gonna be going all night. I don't wanna be in this house all by myself. Why you just can't call me at my mom's?"

"Trina, it's gonna be like two o'clock in the mornin'."

"So?" she hurried.

"Girl, your mom already don't like me."

"So?"

"Yeah, well, maybe."

"What do you mean, 'maybe'? Don't make me hurt you. You better call," she playfully threatened.

Daewoo flashed her a dimpled smile. "I'm just playin'. I'ma call."

"You better." She pulled him to her.

Daewoo allowed Divon to slip slowly to the floor, and hungrily met Trina's kiss. While the four-year-old focused on the T.V. screen, Trina and Daewoo quickly worked themselves horizontally. Without breaking their lip lock, Daewoo pulled the bedspread around them. Trina's body was warm and full, her touch soft and intimate. Daewoo always found himself thoroughly lost in ecstasy during their lovemaking and groaned as he entered her. Rhythmically their strokes met, and their passion became intense. After just seven minutes of pleasure, they both lay spent in each other's arms, tracing fingers across the other's flesh, and watching their son, with his back to them, dance to the purple dinosaur's tune.

Trina turned Daewoo's face to her and smiled. "I'll be here when you get home."

During the walk from 13th & Christian Streets to 6th & Banbridge, Daewoo considered buying a used car. He was tired of walking everywhere be needed to be, and, for a grand, he knew where he'd be able to buy one. By the time he reached "Little Italy," he'd made up his mind to ask Frank for an advance.

Frank was in a booth at the far end of the bar, conversating with two men.

Daewoo took a seat at the bar, where Frank could easily spot him, and ordered a beer. He sat pushing quarters in a newly installed poker machine on the bar top until a hand dropped onto his shoulder.

"Daewoo, glad you made it," Frank greeted.

"I can't afford not to."

"I know. That's why I'm choosing you for this job." Sensing a payday, Daewoo focused on Frank's words.

"I have somethin' set up, Daewoo, where you could make a nice piece of cash. You innerested?"

"Hell yeah," Daewoo stated.

"Good. Grab your beer and join us.

Before Daewoo sat, Frank introduced the men. "Daewoo, this here's Tommy and Bobby Serragucchi.

They're brothers. Tommy, Bobby, this is Daewoo."

Daewoo sat next to Frank, opposite the men.

Tommy was huge with a large head and swollen nose. His skin was pale and his expression serious. Bobby was a slightly smaller build. Right away, Daewoo identified Bobby as the smarter of the two. His eyes were sparkling blue, a man with fair features, except for his top lip curving upward, giving him more of a snarl than a smile. He looked the part of a mafia soldier.

Daewoo eyed the men and wondered what the hell he was getting into. Just a month ago, he was running from shadows; now, he was sharing secrets with mafia soldiers. Who would've guessed, he thought? He settled deeper into his seat, hoping to not say anything stupid or ask too many questions. He'd watched plenty of mafia flicks on television and knew the effectiveness of silence. He listened to Frank speak in his thick, Italian accent.

"Daewoo," Frank said, "Tommy and Bobby have a problem. It seems one of our clients has a debt that needs takin' care of."

"What kind a debt?" Daewoo asked.

"The two-hundred-fifty-thousand-dollar kind," Bobby said.

His cold, blue eyes seemingly stared through Daewoo.

Daewoo returned the man's stare, not wanting to show any sign of weakness.

"Daewoo, I ask you to join us because I think you can help these gentlemen," Frank was saying.

"Me? I don't even know who it is."

"Sure, you do," Frank assured him. "The drop

upstate. The big, white house with all the gates and shit."

"The politician dude?"

"Yeah, him," Frank confirmed.

"What? You need me to pick it up?"

Frank took a sip from his glass.

The Serragucchies followed suit.

"Not exactly," Frank answers. "The Serragucchies came down from Chicago to catch up with Mr. Fontes. Let's just say that somethin' went wrong and now the Councilman has locked himself behind bodyguards and security cameras."

"So, where do I come in?"

"You figure in like this," Frank said. "Besides Mr. Fontes having a gambling problem, he also has a smack problem. You're his supplier, Daewoo, he'll let you through the gate. All we need you to do is park the truck, with our friends here," Frank waved toward the brothers, "stashed in the back, and do your usual deal."

"Are y'all gonna kill 'em?"

"Does it matter?" Tommy asked.

"Yeah, it matter," Daewoo shrieked. "My face'll be all over those tapes."

"Don't worry, I'll get the tapes," Bobby offered.

"And you expect me to rely on that?" Daewoo spat.

"I'm a man of my word," Bobby offered magnanimously then looked to Frank questioningly.

Frank got the message. "Excuse me, Gentlemen," he said. "Daewoo, let me speak to you a sec." Frank guided him to the bar with frustration covering his face.

"What's the matter with you, Daewoo? You fuckin' wimpin' out on me or somethin'?"

Daewoo stood eye to eye with Frank's cutting glare. "Frank, I don't mean no disrespect…I trust you and all…but do you really expect me to trust these guys. For all I know, they could be settin' me up."

"Listen, Daewoo, this is Frank you talkin' to. They gave me their word they wouldn't kill the guy."

"Then why go through bullshit?"

"Don't concern yourself with that. You just do your part, apish?"

Daewoo glared at the two soldiers. "Yeah, I understand."

"Fuck understanding, Daewoo. You can't fuck this up."

Daewoo sensed his job depended on him accepting this assignment. Reluctantly, he nodded. "I'ma trust you, Frank."

"Then you got nothin' to worry about. C'mon before they think you're some kind a pussy."

"One more thing, Frank."

"What now?"

"What's my take on this?"

Frank smirked. "Two G's."

Daewoo masked his excitement. "And all I gotta do is drop these dudes off, huh?"

"That's it."

"I guess frontin' me the money is outta the question?"

Frank peered at Daewoo with concern. "What's this?" he asked. "You know I don't do business like that."

"I know, Frank…it's just that I need a ride. All this walkin' here and there ain't what's up."

Frank paused a second. "I'll think about it."

Later, after the Serragucchies had departed, Daewoo and Frank sat alone in the booth.

"You know, the car thing you spoke about might not be such a bad thing," Frank said. He stirred his drink with a forefinger.

"You think so?"

"Sure. In fact, I got a cousin who could help out."

"I'd appreciate the help, Frank."

"No problem. You just gotta do this thing with the Serraguchies for me."

Daewoo sensed Frank's desperateness. Even as he mouthed the words, "I got you, Frank," he knew the job was something he had to do, not for Frank, but to prove to himself that he was no longer that greedy, paranoid crackhead, who stood by and watched Candy and Paul Montross be murdered. He finished his beer and exited "Little Italy" depressed.

The heat from the earlier sun had cooled, and he hurried to get home to hide his shame between Trina's thighs.

Franklin Park lies smack in the middle of Philadelphia's downtown district. For years, the small park has served as a place of tranquility for many of the surrounding business' employees. The park's fountain, a towering, iron Pegasus, sprayed its usual jets while Tone and Stacey sat at its edge, dangling their feet in its two-foot moat.

During the past month, Tone and Stacey have seen plenty of each other, but today was different. Today was their first date. Tone felt the change was necessary and even stole an all-black Cadillac to make the occasion special. Usually, they'd sink into the project's shadows getting blunted, drinking, or making out. Routinely, the escapades would end with Tone searching out a trick to relieve his lust. He was trying his hardest to be patient with Stacey's inexperience, but, over the past two weeks, his patience has become discouragement, and he hoped today's gesture would ease Stacey's panties down a few more inches.

"Did you enjoy the movie?" Tone asked.

"It was O.K. I didn't like all the killing, though."

"It was only a movie."

"So what? You don't know what fool take that stuff for real," Stacey responded.

"Well, I thought that shit was phat."

"You would, wouldn't you?"

Tone pulled his feet from the water and stood. "Hell yeah! 'Dem niggas was blasting' like crazy."

"Boy, you need to cut it out." She cupped a handful of water and threw it at him. She laughed as he easily dodged it.

Later at Sizzler, when Tone was done his meal, he pushed his plate away and smiled. This was his first glimpse of Stacey eating publicly, and he teased her about each tiny bite and small wipe she applied to her mouth.

"Girl, you need to stop frontin' and eat that food. If your ass was home, you would'a been wolfed that steak down."

"Ain't nobody frontin'," she said defensively. "This is

how I eat."

"Yeah right. I bet." Through a window, Tone watched a police cruiser pass. His mind drifted back to Candy, Daewoo, and why he and Daewoo have not crossed paths since the stickup. He wondered if Daewoo was in jail, and, if so, would he rat. He pondered the idea till Stacey's child-like voice pulled him from his thoughts.

"Excuse me. I'm still here," she remarked.

"Dag, my bad."

"What' s wrong?"

"Nothin'."

"Then what were you thinking about?"

"Just wonderin' 'bout somethin'."

"Like what?"

"Dag, Girl!" he jeered. "Stop being so nosy. You done eatin' yet?"

She rolled her eyes. "Yeah, I'm done."

"Good. Let's get outta here."

"What's wrong with you?" Stacey asked, noticing Tone's attitude had become sour.

Tone caught himself. "Ain't nothin' wrong. Somethin' just been buggin' me lately."

"Well, your face can't get no longer."

"Maybe I just need some T.L.C.?"

She giggled. "Is that where all those bumps on your face come from?"

"What bumps?" Tone touched his forehead.

"Ain't no bumps on your face. I'm just playing."

Tone's face became serious. "Is that why you takin' so long to give that thing up…because you just playin'?"

Stacey's smile disappeared. "We gotta go there again?" she asked.

"Nah, we ain't gotta go there…but you actin' like my lady and all. It's only right you break a brother off."

She stared down at her plate. "I told you I ain't trying to have no babies."

"Is that all?" he replied quickly. "Hell, I ain't got no problem wearing a hat.

"I know you don't. And as soon as you hit, your ass'll probably change."

"Girl, you trippin'."

"I ain't the one that's trippin'," Stacey sneered. Her head swiveled from side to side as she spoke. "Your ass is the one that's trippin'."

Tone's anger had begun to boil. As his thoughts became warped, the small restaurant seemed to swallow them, and Stacey's lips, those beautiful lips, seemed to open and close at lightning speed. Suddenly, as if a steel door had slammed shut all reasoning, Tone watched Stacey's slim body fall backward from her chair, and her small manicured hand grasp at his arm returning. His eyes were hazed and his lips had evolved into a snarl. "BITCH!" he screamed. "DON'T YOUR PUNK-ASS EVER TRY TO CHUMP ME AGAIN! I DON'T KNOW WHO THE FUCK YOU THINK YOU TALKIN' TO! I AIN'T NONE A THOSE 'SUCKA' ASS' NIGGAHS YOU BEEN FUCKIN' WIT'!"

Stacey cringed at the venom in Tone's words. She snatched at her small purse and tried crawling away. Tone was already around the table snatching her up by the shoulders.

He pushed her toward the front exit with an added kick in the ass. "GET THE FUCK OUTTA HERE!" he screamed as the manager of the restaurant rushed toward them. In one motion, Tone snatched the .45 from his waistband and pointed it toward the manager. The man stopped in his tracks. Tone glared at him. "Come on! Be a hero,"

"Tone! No!" Stacey yelled.

Tone turned toward her scream. Her eyes were filled with tears. He turned back to the shaken man at the end of the gun barrel.

The restaurant had become as quiet as a good night's sleep, and the few other employees and customers stood wide-eyed at the horror.

"Consider yourself lucky," Tone advised as he tucked the gun back into his waistband. He snatched Stacey by the arm and pulled her to a trot toward the car. Once there, he practically threw her inside the passenger side. When he leaped into the driver's seat, his features were hard.

"Tone, why you doing this?" she sobbed.

"What did you expect me to do…let 'em hold me till the police showed? I don't think so. I ain't the one." He pulled the car into traffic.

"I hope you taking me home?" Stacey asked testily. Tears of frustration streamed across her chocolate cheeks and dripped from her small chin.

"Where the hell you think I'm takin' you?" Tone shot back.

"Just take me home," she demanded.

"You need to stop actin' like a spoiled ass baby. Like a

little ass slap hurt you."

"Don't hand me that shit, Tone. You don't be putting your fucking hands on me."

Tone shot her an icy glance. "You still talkin' shit?" he questioned.

She folded her arms across her chest and pouted, mumbling under her breath, "Hmm. I ain't no punching bag 'cause you ain't getting no pussy."

"I ain't warning you no more," Tone cautioned.

Stacey thought it best to keep quiet, but resumed her pouting - not out of fear of getting hit again, but out of fear of losing the first "real" boyfriend she's ever had. In the past, Stacey had been able to manipulate boys with her teasing, but now, it seems those days have ended. She watched Tone from the corner of her eye as he drove. She wondered if her mother's reason for Stacey's father hitting Stacey's mother was true. "He only hits me to show me he cares," her mother had said. How sick she thought of her mother, then, but now, with Tone, she understood the circumstances of her mother having allowed it to continue. The fear of loneliness and love. She cursed herself for loving Tone. For not being able to satisfy him sexually. Through her insecurity, she found herself understanding his frustrations to the extent where she wanted to reach across the seat and hold him. She'd no idea it would take so little to upset him. She'd never seen him so strong and forceful - so in control of her, and the situation; but yet, still vulnerable. Surprisingly, she found his rage stimulating. The strength of her man alone has set a fire between her thighs. She crossed her legs to cool the warmth and pulled a small compact from her Gucci handbag. She searched its mirror for visible scars on her face but saw none. All the scars she had encountered were deep inside of her.

Tone pulled the stolen Caddy to the curb at 1241 building. Instead of Stacey leaping from the car as Tone expected her to, she sat staring at her hands folded on her lap. He put the car in park and sat back in his seat with a sigh. "Stacey," he began, "I'm sorry today ain't turn out like I hoped."

"Oh, really?" she sniffed. "Why would you be sorry. You did what you wanted to, didn't you?"

"No. I didn't. And I'm not sorry 'bout slappin' you either. I'm sorry that what I thought was so good, turned out to be wrong."

"Don't hand me that. If you love me, you'd find another way to show it." She pushed open the door, got out, then slammed it close. "Call me when you get your shit together," she called over her shoulder as she stalked into the building.

"What's your name?"

"Stoney Hightower."

"Number?"

"ML-Z635."

"You have your property?"

"Yeah, I got it."

"Good. Follow me."

Stoney followed the huge, pale prison guard through a

narrow corridor to the prison's massive, steel front gate.

"Wait here," the guard ordered.

And Stoney did - just as excitedly as a house-broken K-9 about to be walked.

The guard returned and pressed a black intercom button next to the gate. "Open one!" he barked into a small speaker.

Almost immediately the monstrous front gate slowly opened. Stoney had waited two long years for this moment, and now that it's arrived, the apprehension of leaving one prison for another harassed him. The wind of change that nestled in Stoney was an emotion experienced by many ex-cons in route to a ghetto's combativeness.

Stoney stepped outside of the gate and smiled up at an endless blue sky. Unlike the dirt-filled prison yard he'd become so familiar with over the past two years, a square lawn, manicured and virescent, separated the prison and its parking lot.

After two years of being told to stay off of the grass, Stoney avoided the cemented walkway leading to the parking area and strolled across the lawn, enjoying the sinking cushion beneath his feet.

The lot held close to two dozen vehicles. Next to a near-new Cadillac Sedan Deville, Milton Hightower stood waiting for his son. When Stoney reached him, they embraced.

"It took you long enough. I thought you wanted to stay," Milton joked.

"Thanks for coming to pick me up."

"Well, I figured I left you here long enough." Stoney

smiled. "I knew I was railroaded."

As the Sedan Deville drifted across the back-country road, Stoney settled into the comfortable, red velour seat and enjoyed the ride. He found the passing counties fairy-tale compared to his way of living.

The billows of green pastures and sculpturesque homes. The stifling stench of cow manure, the absence of human activity all contributes to his idea. The stench of manure he could relate to, but the simplism and tranquility were a world away from what he was used to. "What's on your mind, Son?"

"I'm just thinking."

"I know that. That's why I asked."

"I'm thinking about Mom and how much she would've hated living out here."

Milton nodded. "Yeah, that she would've. No card parties.

Nothing to do. Hell, I've given her a week before she'd've hightailed back to Philly."

"That's all?"

"That's about it. That woman was something."

Both men inhaled deeply then sat brooding. Each felt he could peg the other's thoughts.

"Have you spoke to Ryan?" Stoney asked finally.

"Just once."

"What did he say?"

"Nothing really. Just that he'd keep me informed."

"Come on, Pop, you know how cops drag their feet when crimes happen in the ghetto."

Milton turned left onto the freeway. "Stoney, I'm sure

Ryan's doing all he can."

Stoney returned his stare to the passing scenery. "Well, I plan on staying on top of him, now that I'm out."

Milton frowned. "Now don't go and do something stupid. I know you're upset, but Stoney, you gotta let the police handle this."

Stoney's head snapped around. "What do you expect me to do, let whoever did it get away?"

"Negro, please. What do you want…some type of vigilante justice? Revenge is crazy. Just think how it'll be if everyone took revenge on their own. Back and forth it'll go. But when the law catches a killer, the chain is broken, you live and forget."

Stoney looked into his father's eyes. "I'll never forget."

"I know you won't. All I'm asking you to do is not throw your life away by doing something dumb. You know these people ain't got no problem throwing your ass right back where you just came from."

Thoughts of the tiny cell rushed through Stoney's mind. He understood his father's point but knew he would not, regardless if his father was right or wrong, be able to let the police handle things alone. Whatever he chose to do, he thought, he would be careful.

"Are you hungry?" Milton asked.

Stoney took a second before nodding. "A little."

"Good. So am I." Milton squirmed in the driver's seat, hunched over the steering wheel then stomped a heavy foot on the gas pedal. Shortly after noon, Milton pulled the Sedan Deville into one of Richard Allen Project's many courtyards.

Stoney held many memories of the courtyard, good and bad. He searched the row-homes' dilapidated exteriors, recapturing some of those moments.

The courtyard appeared as it did two years ago. The ground still of asphalt and the early afternoon still as sleepy. It looked as if the project's residents have yet to awaken from a night of joyous conflicts and early dawn straggling.

Outside one home, Clara Hightower, Stoney's stepmother, stood as the Caddy headed her way. Before Stoney could exit the car, she was there sporting the lime apron she'd worn when Stone had last saw her. She clasped her palms together, kissed her hands, then tossed it heavenward. "Come on outta there," she beckoned. "Give me some sugar."

Stoney smiled at her eagerness. "How you doing?" Stoney asked. He hugged the short, stocky woman. She reeked of cinnamon. "You two come on in this house and let me fix y'all something to eat."

She hadn't changed, Stoney thought. She'd continuously fussed over Stoney and his father as if they were children.

"Clara, we're fine," Milton replied. We had something on the way."

Her hands flew to her hips and she gave Milton a stern staring. "Milton, now I done told you about eating just anybody cooking!"

Stoney smiled at his father's embarrassment.

"Clara, the man was hungry. What was I supposed to do, let 'em starve?"

She rolled disappointing eyes back to Stoney. "Well,

since you're already full of junk, probably, come on in and rest. I know the ride done wore you out."

Stoney knew the only way to satisfy her was to allow her to make him comfortable. He followed her into the house.

The small living room was spotless and neatly furnished. The same quilted afghans covered the sofa and recliner. Stoney concluded that not much had changed around the small home.

"Stoney I'm sorry about what happened to Candy," Clara said.

"Thanks."

"You know you always have a place right here, don't you?"

"I know."

Milton had fled to the kitchen upon entering the house. He returned to the living room, palming a frosty can of beer. "Clara, I hope you don't plan on talking the man's ear off?"

"Oh, hush," she countered. She returned her attention to Stoney. "So, have you made any plans?"

"A few. Basically, I just want to relax for a while and sort through some things."

"Well, that's understandable after being in that horrible place." Her eyes became distant. She inhaled deeply. "My, where does the time go?"

"Away," Stoney answered, his eyes glued to the gold-framed photos of his stepbrother and stepsister. "How's Marcie and Craig?" he asked.

"Oh, they're fine. Marcie was married, you know. Six

months ago."

"Pop told me."

"Craig… he's away in Kuwait now. Some army thing—"

"The Gulf War," Milton interrupted from his recliner.

"That's right. The Gulf War," she agreed.

"Have you heard from him?"

He was home three months ago. He. writes occasionally."

After forty-five minutes of catching up, Stoney headed to his old bedroom. He wasn't surprised much of the room remained unchanged from when he'd last visited. His stepmother rarely threw anything away and had always made a conscious effort to preserve her children's, including Stoney's childhood and teen memorabilia.

Two huge, Parliament-Funkadelic posters hugged the room's cream-colored walls. Deep-cocoa drapes shut out most of the daylight and shadowed the small stereo, television, and king-sized bed.

The quietness of the room was welcoming. For two years, his mind had run riot about the things he would do once released. Now that he was home, what mattered to him most was finding out who killed his mother. He began telephoning people that may have heard something through their connections. An hour into his calls, his step-mother called for him.

"Yeah," he answered.

"Somebody's here to see you."

Bewildered, he ended his call and wondered who knew he was home. He headed downstairs. Halfway down, he smiled.

Sheila Bank's head was held high. She wondered how she could feel such a stranger around the man she knew best and loved most. Softly she bit her bottom lip to force back her tickling smile. When she saw him, her thoughts drifted back to their jr. high school days. When Stoney sat directly behind her and harassed her constantly. Not until they crossed paths at a neighborhood grocery store did either realize they lived in the same area. That day, Stoney'd walked her home. And for the next year, they were inseparable - until Stoney's junior year of varsity basketball, when girls of all sorts began to flock around him and his priorities changed. Back then, when Stoney was not playing ball, he chased girls. When it was not girls, he was devising schemes to make money. In the ghetto, drugs presented the quickest route to fame, and regardless of how much Sheila had protested Stoney's dealings, but for being in love, she just couldn't pull herself away from him. She knew it was just a matter of time before he'd become caught up in something. But what she did not anticipate; although, the subject of them having a child was discussed, was becoming pregnant with his child - eighteen years later.

Milton Hightower smiled at his wife. He and Clara had learned of their grandson months before he was born. At Sheila's request, they had promised not to tell Stoney until he was out of prison. Everyone agreed that he had enough to deal with just trying to do his time. It was now, as they watched the two embrace, did they second guess their decision. Sheila had promised herself she had not become too emotional when this moment arrived. But when Stoney descended the stairs smiling his wide, lovely smile, she found herself fleeing into his arms and clinging to him like hot grits. She stepped back teary-eyed and blushingly looked away.

"Girl, why you crying?" Stoney asked.

She wiped at her eyes. "Cause it's good to see you. Why do you think?"

Her skin was a deep, shiny tan. She stood five-nine, 115 pounds, and bottom-heavy. Her soft, dark-brown eyes held the deepest regard for Stoney. And as he stared back into her two compassionate pools filled with tears, Stoney knew he'd missed her as well.

"How'd you know I was home?" he asked.

"Your dad."

Stoney looked over to his father, who pretended to be engrossed with television. He then eyed his stepmother. She, too, pretended to busy herself in the small kitchen. He realized he was outnumbered. "Come sit down," he offered. "You want something to drink?"

Sheila took a seat on the sofa. "No. I'm fine."

"You sure?"

"I'm sure. I just came by to introduce you to someone."

Stoney's brow took a quizzical dip. "Introduce me to somebody?"

"Yeah," she sang excitedly.

Stoney stared after her as she bounced from the house with a glancing smile over her shoulder. When she returned, she held the hand of a small boy.

Stoney looked from the child to its mother then back to the child. Without having to ask, he knew who the boy was. It only took common sense to read the emphatic smile plastered on Shelia's face.

Chapter Six

Carl's Barbershop was packed with customers waiting patiently for any of four barber chairs to open. Some browsed through outdated magazines while others, insipidly, soaked in a King Kong classic on a 13" black & white television stationed atop an old Coke box.

Two days have passed since Tone's spoken with Stacey. It seemed obvious, to Tone, that Stacey's telephone calls were being monitored. Each time he'd phone, someone would ask, "Who is this?" He'd then be told, "Stacey's not in. Can I take a message?" He realized, this was a patent brush off, but, surprisingly, instead of being angered, he was slightly amused.

"Next!" a barber called.

Heads turned from the television and rose from outdated mags.

It was Tone's turn. He rested back in the barber's chair while the barber worked and chatted about: who ran numbers, who watered their liquor, and whose wife was the least faithful.

Carl's has always been a headquarters for gossip. A

meeting place for conversationalists, regardless of topic. Meaningful or not, someone always seemed to recite some story. Today was no different. Ironically, with Tone's interest, the conversation surrounded the Montross' murders and Stoney's release from prison.

While an elderly man spoke, flashbacks of the killings raced through Tone's mind. He'd never forget how rude Candy had been to him. How she'd tried to challenge his manhood. But what irked him most was knowing Daewoo had witnessed the killings, and now he seemed to have disappeared.

Tone emerged from Carl's freshly groomed, leery of Stoney's release from prison, but focused and confident about what today's agenda carried - making up with Stacey. He knew she'd be at Sigga's today fetching her nephew from summer camp.

Buried in a deli across from the recreation centre, Tone watched and waited. Fifteen minutes later, he was rewarded when Stacey emerged from the centre, trailing her nephew, who happily skipped a few feet ahead.

When she reached the store, Tone exited the doorway as if their running into one another was coincidental. "Stacey, what's up?" he asked, falling into her slowed, leery pace.

"Oh, God, what do you want?" she replied testily. "I'm comin' from the store."

"Mmm-hmm." She stopped and pivoted toward him. Her hands flew to her small, curved hips. "Tone, what do you want?"

Tone stopped alongside her. "Look, I ain't even gonna fake it. I miss you."

She stared into his slitted eyes.

"I know I was wrong and I promise it'll never happen again."

"I already know that," she agreed, "'cause I ain't got time to be nobody's punching bag."

"Girl, you know I don't even think of you that way," he soothed. "I made a mistake. Baby, can't you just forgive me?"

"I'll think about it," she barked as she stormed away.

Tone watched her perfected switch as she bounced away. On a scale of one to ten, he'd give her an eight. She was definitely stacked in the right places. He bolted after her realizing he was about to let his first love walk away. He caught up to her and spun her by the arm. "Listen, Stacey, I know I messed up, but I do care about you a lot." He paused and looked to the clear sky, as if God should help, then back to Stacey. "Baby, I'm sorry. I don't know what I was thinkin' 'bout. It's just…it's just that…I be wantin' you so much and it seem like…like…you be playin' games."

"Well, I don't."

"I didn't say you was. I said it seem."

"Yeah, well, whatever. I gotta go."

"I know. I ain't tryin' to hold you up," he lied. "Is it cool if I call the crib later?"

"You can if you want," she answered stoically. She turned and hollered to her nephew not to stray too far.

"I know you settin' me up."

"Setting you up?"

"Yeah. Every time I called, they said you wasn't home."

"I probably wasn't." A slight smile escaped her.

"Oh, you think that's funny, huh?"

"No."

"Then why didn't you answer my calls?"

"For what? To give you another chance to humiliate me in public?"

"Come on, Stacey, I'm tryin' to make up for that."

"Well, it's gonna take a lot more that a sad face to make me forget what you did…and where'd you get that gun?"

"I been had it."

"Then why I ain't never seen it?"

"Don't worry 'bout that. I plan on gettin' rid of it anyway."

"You need to, bad as your temper is."

Tone had no intention of being lectured about his temper and changed the subject. "So, what's up? We goin' out tonight?"

"I don't know. I said you can call."

Stacey'd already decided to forgive Tone the night he'd slapped her. All she really wanted was an apology and to make him sweat. She loved him. Her first love. And in her childish, naive way of reasoning, she believed him to be truly sorry for what he'd done.

"I guess I gotta go to the movies by myself, huh?" Tone trilled.

"No. You don't. Meet me in front of 1241 about 3:30."

Later, after a struggle to get through Stacey's choice of movie, Tone was finding the rewards of his suffering well worth it. In the front seat of a stolen Town car, parked on a small, deserted street, he slipped a probing hand beneath Stacey's blouse.

"Stop, Tone," Stacey muttered between gasps for air.

"For what?" He met Stacey's stare with disbelief. "Come on, Stacey, don't start this shit again."

"Start what?" she snapped affronted.

Tone pulled his hand from beneath her blouse and snatched a blunt from the dashboard. "I ain't even gonna trip," he grumbled. He lit the blunt and inhaled deeply. When he spoke, large puffs of smoke escaped with his words. "I thought this shit was settled?"

"Is that what you thought?" she drawled, rolling her brown eyes at his gull.

"Look, I ain't tryin' to argue 'bout it. I just thought you was ready to take that next step."

"And what…give you some?"

Tone felt the tension building between them. He shut his eyes tight and laid his head on the headrest. "Whatever," he dismissed. "Here. You want some 'a this?"

"No."

"I guess you don't smoke weed no more either, huh?"

"Yeah. I just don't want none."

For a second, Tone felt like reaching across the seat and strangling her. Instead, he again puffed angrily from the blunt and contemplated her stubbornness.

Stacey looked upon the tightening of Tone's jawline confident he'd not slap her again. She wondered how long she'd be able to use her sexuality to control him. Her thoughts drifted back three years ago when she first discovered her sexuality, a time when she'd watched her older sister and her sister's girlfriends conform to welfare and unsavory men for monetary support in order to raise their children. At thirteen, the adolescent surges of sexuality had gripped her. Masturbation had become Stacey's favorite past time, and lately, three years later, she found herself masturbating even more. She ached to make love to Tone. To finally lose her virginity. Her fear of becoming pregnant nearly trumped her fear of not being any good at pleasing a man. She touched his arm lightly. "Tone, I'm sorry you got the wrong idea."

"Don't even worry 'bout it," he replied dully, without lifting his head from the headrest or opening his eyes. Disappointment covered his face. He took another drag from the blunt. "I'm gettin' used to you teasin' the hell outta me. I'm startin' to think you like this shit." His statement was more a question than an accusation.

"No, I don't."

"I can't tell."

Stacey shyly turned her head away. "I'm just not ready to go there yet."

"It's been over two months. How long do you expect me to wait?"

Tone watched as she took two deep drags. He felt she was testing his manhood just as Candy had done. Enraged, his idea of taking no shorts had begun to surface. Without a word, he started the car and screeched from the curb believing he had a trick for her ass.

❖ ❖ ❖

Stoney had been avoiding this day. The day he'd have to enter the apartment where his mother and stepfather had been gunned down. He struggled emotionally just to turn the key in the lock. The place no longer felt like home. He felt like a visitor entering a carnival's haunted house. He slow-walked the apartment's hallway, pausing at his mother's bedroom, trying to fight through the images of what had occurred. Although he hadn't seen what had taken place, clear images were embedded in his mind.

The lingering scent of disinfectant hung heavy in the apartment, but to Stoney, the smell hardly mattered; the apartment would forever be tainted with blood.

The sound of water running lured him toward the bathroom. He walked light, barely applying the full weight of his muscular frame to each step. The bathroom hung from the living room's edge, giving him a clear view of its door swinging open. He smiled at the salt and pepper haired woman shuffling towels across one arm.

Her face was heavily made up and her yellow, floral house-coat hung loosely just above the floor. "Ooh," she shrieked when she noticed Stoney standing there smiling. "Man, what's wrong with you scaring me like that?"

"I'm sorry, Aunt Millie, I didn't know you were here."

"Come 'ere and give me a hug." Her words dragged, shook, but boomed with strength and authority.

Stoney had forgotten the huge amounts of perfume she wore. He cut the hug short and held the woman at arm's length, "I see you still pack it on," he teased.

She backhanded a smile. Her small, coal eyes sparkled. Just as quick as they glittered, they became watered.

"Come on, Aunt Millie, don't start crying. You know my mom would cuss you out if she knew you wouldn't be strong for us."

She patted her dripping eyes with a towel. "I know, Stoney.

"I know. But why her? She ain't done nothing to deserve what they did."

"I wish I knew. Hopefully, we'll get some answers soon." He planted a small kiss on her forehead.

After taking the time to pack some of his belongings, Stoney sat in his bedroom, sulking. An enormous part of him had been snatched away, not just any piece, the one piece that's meant the most to him. He wondered if his mother had ever met her grandson.

Probably so, he thought. It seems like everyone knew about the child but him. Maybe, he believed, the time has come for him to settle down and raise a family. He knew decisions would have to be made. This he was certain of.

Stoney placed two heavy-duty plastic bags of clothes at the front door and sauntered into the living room.

Aunt Millie was parked on the sofa, hunched forward, shouting back at the Ricki Lake Show, her cracked skin revealing the sufferings she's gone through throughout her sixty-nine years.

"I'm about ready to go," Aunt Millie.

"You leaving so soon?" she asked wonderingly.

"Yes, ma'am. I don't think I could stay here." His eyes were apologetic. He turned away from her, ashamed he lacked her strength.

She raised a wrinkled hand in allegiance. "You don't

have to say a thing. I understand…though I think runnin' from a ghost ain't gonna help."

"I'm not running. It's just…I don't know…strange being here, that's all." He leaned over and pecked her leathery face. "I'll stop by tomorrow and check on you, all right?"

She sat straight-backed and proud. "Son, you ain't gotta be checkin' up on me. I'll be fine."

"I know that. I'm just worried about you staying here."

"Well, don't. I'll be fine."

"You sure?"

"Ain't that what I said? I ain't live this long without knowin' anything better."

The subway ride to Richard Allen project took less than fifteen minutes. Within an hour, Stoney had showered, changed, and managed to get the keys to his father's Caddy.

Stoney rode Broad Street the entire ride back down 13th Street. He parked the Cadillac directly across the street from 13th Street Lounge. He knew there were three places information could be found. Scorpio's, Amityville, and The Lounge. The Lounge was dim. It took several seconds before Stoney's eyes adjusted to the lighting. The sounds of Stevie Wonder's "*Rhythm in the Sky*" chimed from the jukebox. He recognized a few patrons on barstools and in booths. A Bowl-a-Matic occupies one side of the door, a cigarette machine the other. Not much has changed. He smiled at Lydia Phillips still holding court at the bar's rear, and Junior, Manny, and Big Al holding their positions near the door - for business reasons, he assumed.

Big Al was the first to roll his 340-pound frame from a stool and wobble over to Stoney, hand outstretched. "Stoney! My mutherfuckin' man! What's goin' on? I heard a nigga was sprung."

Stoney shook his hand.

The two went back a long way, but, somehow, the love Stoney had had for the fat man seemed lost. "No, I'm not all right," Stoney answered. "You see Monty?"

"Yeah, yeah. He just stepped off a few minutes ago with—"

"Stoney!" Junior interrupted. His shout drew the entire bar's attention to Stoney. "What's up, family?" he continued. "Ain't nothing to it. I see you haven't budged since I been down."

"And I ain't tryin' to either. Hell, business do me just fine sittin' here on my ass."

Following suit, Manny welcomed Stoney home as well. "You want a beer or something?" Manny asked.

"I'm cool. Thanks." Stoney realized that this was the first time he'd thought about drinking since being home. He threw a huge arm around Big Al's shoulder. "Al, let me holler at you for a sec." He separated himself and Al from the others. "Where'd you say Monty went?"

"Him and Reynard left twenty minutes ago with two hoes."

"You know if he cornin' back this way?"

"He ain't say."

"Fuck!" Stoney muttered. "Dig this…You gonna be here when he shows, right?"

"Yeah."

Stoney borrowed a pen from the bartender and scribbled his number on a cocktail napkin. "Here. Give him my number and tell him to get with me. It's important."

"No problem."

"Hey, Stonneyy!" a woman caroled.

Stoney turned to see Lydia Phillips waving him over.

Big Al smiled. "There she go," he kidded. He patted Stoney twice on the back then retreated to his stool.

Stoney and Lydia's relationship has been on and off since high school. She'd been blessed with good looks, everyone says, considering her three brothers and two sisters were true to the word ugly. Although she'd put on a few pounds, Stoney could already tell she hadn't changed. She was still a drunk.

"Hey, you," Stoney greeted, eyeing her finger the neck of a Heineken, "you still looking good I see."

She stood and extended both arms, gesturing. "Don't I get a kiss, a hug or something?"

"You ain't give me a chance," he lied, embracing her.

"You want a drink?" Her mahogany eyes were already glazed.

"Nah. That's O.K."

"How 'bout somethin' else?" she teased.

He smiled down at the woman. "Don't tempt me," he toyed.

She stepped back and playfully slapped at him. "You probably wasn't even gonna call and tell me you was home, was you?"

"Of course, I was. I just had some things to take care of."

"I bet I can guess what one of 'em was?"

"Well, you know I don't kiss and tell, so, you just go right ahead and keep guessing."

Lydia's jealousy had been the main reason for their separations. Her drinking Stoney could deal with, but her jealous rages usually ended with Stoney sustaining injuries. He had to admit her firry nature had always excited him, but now he felt he needed something much more settling. To look at her now, her drinking made her just as ugly as her siblings.

"So, when can I expect our catchup time to start?" asked Lydia.

"Catchup time? Is that what it's called?" Stoney asked, no longer intrigued with her copper-toned skin and jet black, shoulder-length hair.

"No. But we do have a history. Or has it been that bad?"

Stoney shook his head no.

"Then what?"

"I have a lot of stuff to work out right now."

"Like what? Fuckin' some other bitch?" she spat.

Stoney released a disappointed sigh. "Lydia, look, I ain't about to argue with you about who I'm hittin', so I'ma leave you to your beer and whatever else your drinking."

"I'm not arguing."

"Not yet, but you're about to start."

"Ha! You think so?"

"Ha! I know so," he mimicked, standing up and kissing her on the cheek. "Baby, I gotta go right now. Your number's still the same?"

"Mm-hm."

"I'll call you then."

"Whatever, Stoney," she called, her words chasing his back.

Stoney chatted with a few others before leaving the bar. Everyone seemed clueless about who'd killed his mother. He was surprised that so little people even knew who Paul was. For all Stoney knew, he could be befriending a co-conspirator. Until he was certain, he was content on keeping everyone at arm's length.

He sat behind the wheel of the Sedan Deville relieved. He'd felt uncomfortable inside The Lounge with the boosters, dope dealers, and alcoholics. Before prison, the bar was where he'd spent most of his time. Now, unable to shake free the rust of institutionalization, he knew a readjustment period would be necessary.

He parked the Caddy two doors from the pub at 6th & Banbridge. He entered the small dive and headed straight to its rear, where Frank Russo was holding court.

Stoney and Frank had met five years ago when Stoney had worked as a bouncer at a Society Hill nightclub called the "Ritz." A bouncer's salary did nothing for Stoney during those days, but the connections he was able to establish, through drug dealings, made his salary meaningless.

When two Italians tried to muscle in on his sales, it was Frank who'd stepped in and ended what nearly became a bloodbath. Stoney had never understood why Frank had d mediated the incident until he'd been recruited, by Frank, to deliver packages across the Tri-State. It was then, he'd realized, Frank's bigger plan. Frank had needed drivers.

Three middle-aged Italians were sharing a booth with Frank, each busting a gut while hanging onto Frank's every word. Stoney reached the booth and stopped. All eyes turned to him and the laughter slowly subsided.

Frank stopped mid-sentence. "Out-fuckin'-standing," he gushed, staring up at Stoney.

Stoney smiled. "Look at you, Frank. Still tellin' lies?"

"Lies? What the fuck you mean lies? I ain't never tol' nothin' but the truth. Honest to God," he joked, raising his hand in oath.

This brought forth more laughter from the group. "I heard you was out," said Frank.

"You heard right."

Frank's expression became serious. "If you ask me, you never shoulda been there. The motherfucker had it cornin'. Am I right?"

"You shoulda been my lawyer."

"Nah," Frank dismissed. "I gotta fear 'a courtrooms. You shoulda called me though, I mighta been able to do somethin' for ya."

Stoney shrugged. "It's cool, Frank. I do need to talk to you, though."

"Yeah. Sure. Give me a minute to finish up here. We'll take a walk. Get somethin' to eat."

"I'll be out front."

On the second floor of "Jim's Steaks," Stoney and Frank occupied a window seat, allowing them to look down on the South Street crowd going about their shopping.

"It's good to see you back where you belong," Frank commented.

"It feels better than it looks."

Each man pulled the foil from around his cheesesteak hoagie and showered on salt and pepper.

"So how long do you think it'll be before you're ready to come back to work?" Frank asked.

"Now, if you need me."

Frank took a monstrous bite of his steak sandwich and gave a satisfied nod. "Good…good," he managed around a mouthful of sandwich. "I got somethin' easy for you to start with."

"You ain't gotta pull no punches for me, Frank. I need the money. You can save that easy shit for the rookies."

"I know that. I figure you'd wanna start slow."

"Well I don't."

"That's really good," Frank agreed. "Now eat your steak. I paid cash for these."

Little Italy was jumping. People were packed around the cherry wood bar and filled every booth in the place. Those standing smiled while chattering through a smothering of cigarette smoke. Tony Bennett echoed a love tune from the jukebox, and a few elderly Italian couples were enjoying themselves as they danced.

Frank Russo was at his usual booth. Across the table sat the Serragucchi brothers. To Frank's inside, a fellow Daewoo had never met.

Frank's lips flapped continuously. No doubt, Daewoo believed he was exaggerating a story because the others listened attentively. The four men paid Daewoo's arrival little attention. When the jukebox paused between songs, the group's laughter seemed to rise from festive to rude.

Daewoo glanced around, slightly embarrassed. No one else seemed bothered. He waited till Frank showed interest in him standing there before speaking. "What's happening', boss man?"

"Ah, Daewoo, ya made it," Frank drawled in his heavy Italian accent. He waved a glass of clear liquor at the man Daewoo didn't know. "This here's Mario. He's gonna do the drivin' tonight. Apish?"

"Whatever, Frank. It don't matter to me who drive."

"Good." Frank nodded. "And of course, you remember your passengers." Frank waved the same glass at the Serragucchies.

The two men nodded in unison.

Daewoo nodded back. He'd a deep, gut feeling about the brothers, sort of like stomaching a bowl of rotten worms. He turned back to Frank. "So, where's the truck?"

"It'll be here. No need going to the depot tonight, mean- time…grab a brewski."

Daewoo strolled to the bar wrinkling his brow over whether his newfound connection would carry the promises he'd hoped. He ordered a Budweiser. Perhaps things have changed for the better, he reasoned. He was off cocaine and making money. Trina was back with him. Now, all he'd to do was this thing for Frank to add another positive to his life. A car.

Two beers later, a leggy brunette whispered in Frank's ear. When she'd disappeared, Frank turned to Daewoo. "The truck's out back."

Daewoo trailed Frank, Mario, and the Serragucchies out through the bar's back door.

The truck was of medium size with a logo emblazoned on its side, which read:

WESTMONT CABLE SERVICE PENNSYLVANIA'S FIRST CHOICE (719-555-3000)

Mario hurriedly leaped into the driver's seat and revved the engine. The small alleyway provided plenty of seclusions for the Serragucchies to pull black overalls over their clothes.

Daewoo noticed the silver .44 magnums stuffed in their shoulder holsters.

"Here you go," Frank said.

Daewoo turned his attention to the thick, beige envelope. "What's this?"

"I'ma be outta town a coupl'a days. This here's for the job."

Daewoo pocketed the envelope against the urge to open it. "You just remember to do the exact thing you been doing."

"No sweat."

"I'm serious, Daewoo. Don't fuck this up. It means a lot to me. And tell your Mexican partner the same thing."

The envelope of cash eased Daewoo's mind during the ride to the Fontes estate. Mostly he daydreamed about the type of car he'd purchase.

They reached the estate shortly before 10 p.m. The front gate was huge, towering more than fifteen feet with a ten-foot wall extended around the property. A host of still cameras were affixed every hundred feet or so.

"You know what to do?" Bobby Serragucchi asked.

"Yeah, I got it. Relax."

He watched the brothers pull aside two large metal trunks that appeared to be bolted to the truck's bed; spaces large enough to conceal the men were revealed. When the Serragucchies were hidden, Mario eased the truck to the front gate next to an intercom and between two cameras.

Just inside the gate, twenty feet away, was a booth, occupying a uniformed guard, whose voice echoed through the intercom. He ordered Mario to shut off the truck's engine.

Mario did so.

"What can I do for you?" the voice crackled.

Daewoo hung from the window and spoke into the speaker. "Uh, yeah. Mr. Fontes is expecting us."

"Your name?"

'Stokes," Daewoo answered.

"I'll need to see some I.D."

"ID?" Daewoo squealed. "I never had to show I.D. before."

"I don't know what to tell you," the guard replied.

Daewoo recalled the incident in Saigon where he needed I.D. to enter the building. "Here we go again," he mumbled, recalling Frank's words, *'Don't fuck this up, Daewoo,"* as well. He frowned. "Look, sir, I don't have any I.D., but, if you call your boss and have him take a look, I'm sure this'll all be straightened out."

"I'm sorry, but I'm under strict orders here."

Daewoo was irritated. "Look," he replied firmly, "I'm on the list, right?"

"That's not the problem."

"Then what is? Call Mr. Fontes and let him decide. If you don't…you might find yourself out of a gig." Daewoo could see the guard clearly from where he sat. He felt the daggered stare the man gave him before reaching for the telephone.

Daewoo sighed relief.

"Where you fuckin' I.D., mon?" Mario asked.

"I don't carry none."

"How somebody know who you be?"

Daewoo ignored the question and eyed the guard. A bit after a minute, the gate partially opened, and the guard emerged.

He was built scrawny, mid-forties with an owl face and baggy, tan uniform. In his right hand, he lugged a canary-yellow flashlight. "I'm gonna have'ta look in the back. Can you open it up, please?"

Daewoo stepped from the truck and pulled up the retractable door.

The truck's bed contained the two metal trunks, some thick, black cables, a few satellite disks, and tools.

Satisfied, the guard returned to the booth, "You can go," the intercom squawked as the huge gate slid open.

Twenty minutes after entering the Fontes estate, Daewoo and Mario were headed back to Philly, minus the Serragucchies. Not everything had gone as usual. Daewoo had noticed, almost immediately, the extra security that had surrounded the spacious home. The security had been mostly targeted toward the mansion, and he'd no problem directing Mario's angling of the truck's rear out of the camera's view. Another change had been the unfriendliness in the man's eyes, who Daewoo consistently delivered the packages to. The man had been overly anxious to conclude their business, and two other men with bulged jackets had flanked the man this time. Daewoo had felt extremely fortunate to have gotten out of there alive.

No sooner Mario turned onto Broad Street, Daewoo had him drop him off at a center city pub.

"Another one, Mack?" the bartender asked dutifully.

"As quick as this one is empty," Daewoo replied. He gulped the remains of his third straight Smirnoff and spun on the black leather stool.

The long, narrow bar hung from the wall farthest from the front door. A large pool table dressed in a forest-green, velour top was its centerpiece. Two young, white men, preppy types, occupied the table. The crowd was chatty, twenty or so patrons. Ten sat around tiny, circular oak tables with assortments of condiments in their centers. The walls were lined with plastic brick paneling hosting paintings of monstrous oceanic waves and beached landscapes. And in one corner, a forty-two-inch color T.V. hung, volume turned down, displaying the 11:30 broadcast of Channel 7 news. *Nothing like the ghetto bars,*

Daewoo thought. He'd rather do his drinking elsewhere. He turned to the bartender. "What I owe you?"

"Twelve even."

He plucked his tab from his bankroll and tossed it onto the bar top. As he turned to leave, he caught a glimpse of the T.V. broadcast and froze. Although the volume was down, Daewoo had a clear idea what the news report was about.

Outside the Fontes estate, a female reporter, with strong Asian features, stood giving, what seemed to Daewoo, an animated accounting of what had occurred. Daewoo ached to holler to someone to turn up the volume, but when his and Mario's pictures were aired, he cringed, not wanting to draw attention to himself. The broadcast concluded with footage of several body-bags being lifter into coroners' wagons.

Without a glance backward, Daewoo hurried from the pub, stopping only when he realized his running would draw attention. He swiftly treaded through the night, allowing the cool, night air to clear his thoughts. "Lucky streak my ass!" he exclaimed as he picked up the pace toward 13th Street. He stopped abruptly and cursed. The police would surely be waiting for him to show his mug in the projects. "I'm fucked," he grumbled through clenched teeth. Angrily, he punched the heal of his left palm. "I knew I shouldn't a trusted those no good mother-fuckers! I knew it! I knew it!" Daewoo bitched and stomped two more blocks before spotting a phone booth. He fished out a quarter and dialed Frank's number. The line rang three times before an answering machine beeped in. "Frank, if you there, pick up." Daewoo's voice quaked as he spoke. "Frank, you there? Pick up." He paused a few seconds to peer up and down the street. He cupped the mouthpiece as if his words would escape the booth. "Frank, listen. I don't know when you'll get this message, but don't leave town. There's been some kind of mix up. I'ma meet you at the bar as soon as it open." He slammed down the receiver. As an afterthought, he snatched up the receiver, dropped in another coin and called Trina. Six rings went by. "Come on, baby," he prayed, "pick up the phone."

Nothing. He hung up, retrieved his quarter, and stepped from the booth, knowing he needed a place to hide till morning.

Tone swung the Town car onto the side of the road. He laid his head on the headrest and regretted having to get rid of the .45. He picked the gun up from the passenger seat and stroked its barrel. He'd miss the security of having the gun, but it was time to get rid of it. He tucked the gat into his waistband and jogged to the riverbank.

Evening had long ago peeked from behind the day's activities, and picture-postcard-like, the Schuylkill River effortlessly riveted by. He hurled the gun as far as he could. When it plopped into the water, he swore he heard his father's voice murmur, *"Good job, son."* If only he could have heard that voice earlier and listened to it more often, he thought, maybe he'd have not done what he'd done to Stacey earlier in the day. He'd had enough of Stacey's sexual teasing and had made up his mind that today would be the day she'd regret her childish game. He'd driven slowly through Fairmont Park to a desert- ed Smith Playground where, as a child, he'd encountered some of his more enjoyable moments.

"Where we are going, boy?" Stacey had asked, turning down the music to finally break her silence, a lasting silence since they'd entered the park.

"I got somethin' to show you," Tone had replied. "Back here?"

He'd looked at her innocently. "Yeah. Back here."

"Tone, I ain't even for it right now."

"Girl, chill. Turn the radio back up," he'd replied.

The deeper into the park Tone had drove, the more distrust Stacey had shown. She twisted to peer out of each window in hopes of a peek of this something Tone had to show her.

He turned the radio volume down just before entering an area marked with a large white sign with red lettering: "**NO TRESPASSING**," the sign read.

Stacey read the sign. "Uh-uh, Tone. Let me out of this car, right now." She reached for the door handle.

"What? You gonna jump outta the car? Just chill…damn. You act like you don't trust me."

She released the door handle. "Should I?"

Tone ignored her. He turned onto a small, dirt road leading to the parking area, pulled into the lot and shut off the engine.

Curious, Stacey again twisted her head from side to side, searching for what Tone had said he wanted to show her. She shot a disgusted stare at him. "See, I knew your ass was lying," she barked.

Tone smiled. He nonchalantly retrieved a half-filled

sandwich bag of weed from his pants pocket and tossed it onto her lap. "Here. Roll this up."

Stacey eyed the bag. "Is this all you think about?"

"No. Just roll it up.

"She fingered the bag as believe you brought me all the way out here to get high."

"I guess I'm tired of the jets. Since meeting Stacey, Tone's had to quell his burning lust for her. And now, as her white, cotton mini-skirt rode high on her thick dark thighs, his eyes roamed over the sixteen-year-old's satiny skin. Lustfully, he licked his lips at her clasped knees preventing the sandwich bag from spilling over. He imagined himself between her thighs; inside her young, sexy body.

He continued staring at her apply saliva to the blunt with her tongue, rolling it in her mouth as if it were a taffy.

She must have felt his stare. "What's wrong with you?" she asked, reaching for the car's lighter. She pushed it in.

"Ain't nothin' wrong. I'm checkin' you out."

"Mm-hm. You probably calling me all kinds'a bitches."

"Nah, nothin' like that. I'm wonderin' how long you gonna play wit' the weed."

She sucked her teeth. "Boy, ain't nobody playing with no refer."

The car lighter popped out. Stacey reached for the lighter, forcing her long, erect nipples to strain against her thin, cotton blouse.

Tone resisted grabbing her. Instead, he looked away until she passed him the blunt - their third of the day. He noticed her eyes were near closed and her movements slow and awkward.

"Here," he said, offering her more of the half-smoked blunt.

She waved a weary hand. "I don't want no more." She leaned an elbow on the armrest and rested her head in her palm.

"You cool?" Tone asked. He stumped the blunt in the ash-tray and reached for her thigh. "Come on, girl," he coaxed. He slid closer to her. "You high as hell ain't you?"

She pushed his probing hand from beneath her skirt. "I ain't that high," she shot back.

Tone laughed it off. "Oh, no?"

"No."

"Then give me a kiss." "For what?"

"Oh, now I need a reason to get a kiss?"

"No."

"Then give me a kiss then," he said pointedly. He turned her head toward him and placed his lips to hers. It was a soft kiss. A kiss with just enough intensity to warrant another, one that urged him to explore farther. He scooted even closer to her, sure to not interrupt the moment. Skillfully, he maneuvered her horizontal and climbed on top of her. Her scent was intoxicating. Fresh. Innocent. Her body, loose and inviting as she squirmed beneath him. He reached beneath her blouse and freed one perfect breast from her bra. Soft, firm and warm it felt in his palm. She moaned. Her hips seemed to rise and meet his pelvis and her eyes rolled back into her head, revealing ghostly white slits. Then she stopped.

"Uh-uh, Tone," she murmured with glazed eyes. "Stop."

Tone continued. Today was the day, he'd decided that he'd no longer have to wonder about the tightness and warmth of her.

Like a freshly caught trout, she wiggled beneath him, this time trying to break free. "I said stop!" she screamed, her high seemingly lost. She pushed at his shoulders.

Tone's intensity rose. He pinned both her arms above her head and continued his mauling.

"Please don't," she begged. She broke free an arm and pushed up on his chin.

He recaptured the arm. "Come on, Stacey, stop playin'. You know you want to."

"No, I don't," she sobbed. Tears had begun to flow from her eyes. She again broke free an arm, this time, she angrily swung at his face.

The sound of the smack seemed to linger forever inside the Town car. Both stopped wrestling and stared at the other.

"Bitch!" Tone yelled. "That's how you want it?" He pushed a forearm down on her throat. "Shut the fuck up!" he snarled.

He reached beneath the seat for the .45 caliber and pointed it to her face. "Now what?" His words were venomous. "You think I'm playin'?" He dug beneath her skirt and tore away her white laced panties.

"No, Tone. Please don't do this!"

Tone's eyes were cold. He placed the gun barrel to her head and violently shoved a forefinger deep inside of her. He became even more excited when he discovered her vagina was hot and surprisingly hairless.

"No!" she screamed, fighting to twist to her side and tighten both legs together. Without regard to the gun, she continued to fight and claw.

Frustrated, Tone cocked his arm back and slapped her flush across the cheek. Instantly, her fighting ceased and just as quickly, Tone's sexual frustration subsided.

The voice was too late.

Stacey covered her face with both hands and cried.

Tone, finally aware of what he'd done, had slowly lifted from atop of her. He'd sat still in the driver's seat, staring blankly at the gun. He'd paid no mind to Stacey, who'd bolted from the car, screaming threats of police and repercussions.

Instead, he'd thought of how his father's spirit must be scouring down on him. Without a word or thought of apologizing to Stacey, he started the car and tore from the lot. And now, standing worrisome, reading the Schuylkill waters, he wondered about his next move. One thing was for certain, he believed, he'd have to avoid 13th Street for a while. He knew Stacey was pissed off enough to go to the police; if so, then going home was also out of the question.

The trip across East River Drive had taken minutes. The late-evening traffic was light, allowing Tone time to conjure a place to lay low. He pulled the Lincoln onto Rater Street and parked a few doors from Scorpio's. Even before Tone exited the car, loud talking and laughter carried the night's message and anticipation stirred inside of him. He dug in his front jeans pocket and retrieved a crumpled fifty-seven bucks. He counted off ten for a room and forty for get-high. He'd make a night of it, he thought. In the morning, he'd off the Lincoln.

Chapter Seven

The bedroom's thick, cocoa-brown drapes shut out the daylight. The only light illuminating Stoney's bedroom flickered from the 24" color television. Stoney quickly flipped through its channels. Next to him lie his newfound son, belly-down, sucking air from a near-empty baby bottle. Stoney eased the bottle from the child's mouth. "Your grandmother would've loved you," he whispered. He was certain she'd have. She'd made her desire to be a grandmother known years before her death. He swirled his fingers in the child's soft, curly hair and recalled yesterday's visit with Ryan.

The two had met for lunch at the Wagon Train, an 18th Century railroad car that had been converted into a diner, two blocks from City Hall.

After sparring down memory lane, Stoney had switched the conversation to Paul's and his mother's deaths.

"Stoney, I'm still trying to make sense of this thing," Ryan had said. "What went down at your mom's place, we know was robbery. Did you know that she was still dealing?"

"Yeah, I knew."

"Did Paul have any enemies that you know of?"

Stoney thought for a moment. "He stayed home mostly. Sometimes he played chess over Sigga's."

A curvy waitress interrupted them with the check then bounced away.

"I gotta tell you, Stoney, this case bothers me."

"Why?"

"Because anyone could've done it. Hell, we found fifty sets of prints in the apartment's hallway alone."

"Did you check 'em?"

Ryan picked a napkin up from the table, wiped his hands and dropped it in his plate, insulted. "Of course, we checked them."

"So, you telling me you got nothing?"

"No. That's not what I'm saying."

"Then what?"

Ryan breathed deeply before leaning forward. "Look, I have no business telling you this, but there may be a witness."

"A witness. Somebody that saw it you mean?"

"Not exactly." Ryan leaned back in his seat. "She's been in a coma over a month."

"A month? What makes you think she saw anything?"

"She was shot with the same gun a few hours later."

The waitress returned smiling and carried off their empty plates. When she was out of earshot, Ryan continued. "Look, this case may take some time. I've been showing this witness mugshots for days. She still can't recall the suspects' names.

"It's more than one person?"

"From what we know, there were two guys."

"And you think she can identify 'em?"

"The doctor says we gotta give her mind time, so, 'till then, all I can do is continue looking for leads."

Ryan stood and dropped two tens onto the tabletop. "I'm headed back to work. You know how to reach me. My treat."

"Yeah. Sure," Stoney replied, grateful.

Before Ryan turned away, he'd looked at Stoney with all seriousness. "Stoney, don't think I'll hesitate to lock your ass up if you try to be a hero."

Stoney had smiled. "I see you still have a sense of humor."

"I'm serious, Stoney."

"I know you are."

"Then I have your word you'll let us handle this?"

Stoney had looked away then back to his friend. "All I want is justice."

"So do I, Stoney. So do I."

Stoney had left the dining car confident Ryan wouldn't allow the case to fade away, but certainly more could be done. He clicked off the television and reached for the telephone. He had two calls to make. The first to The Lounge. After two rings, a man answered.

"Is Monty around?" Stoney asked.

"I don't know. Let me check."

A minute later, he returned. "Nope. He ain't here."

"How 'bout Big Al?"

"Yeah, Al's here."

Stoney listened to the background chatter until Al's

deep voice came onto the line. "Al, this here's Stoney. Did you give Monty my message?"

"Oh, hey, Stoney. Nah, I ain't see Monty yet. The word is, he's over A.C."

"A.C.?"

"That's what I hear. You remember I tol' you 'bout those two ho's he left with right…? Well, I found out they was Mackey White's. You know Mackey - the pimp - over 16th Street? Anyway, they decided to clip Mackey for two grand. You know the deal…ho's wanted to smoke…Monty had the coke, so he rolled wit' 'em. I guess he'll show when the ho's go broke."

"I guess my partner still ain't change, huh?"

"Neither has the coke game," Al added.

"Well, when he does show, holler at me. Cool?"

"I got you."

Stoney hung up and dialed Shelia's number. So far, she and his son, Jamal, have been his most pleasant surprises since returning home.

Sheila's mother answered the phone in her recognizable hoarse tone.

"Is Sheila in?" Stoney asked.

"Don't you say hello?" she snapped. "Sheila's not the only one living in this house."

"I'm sorry, Mrs. Banks. How are you?"

She didn't answer, which was fine with him. He was sick of receiving condolences about his mother's death anyhow. To him, most people's concerns were bullshit anyway - the proper thing to say before asking a lot of dumb-ass questions for which he had no answers to.

Sheila's voice came on the line. "Hello."

"Hey, it's me."

"What's wrong?"

"I'm bored."

"Already? Just be glad you don't have to babysit these three over here. They never sleep."

"Well, that's all Jamal's done."

"Whaaat?" she drawled. "That bad ass don't take naps for me."

Stoney laughed. "It's a man thing, sweetheart."

"Yeah? Well, when little man wakes up, tell him his mommy loves him."

Stoney looked to his son. "I was hoping you'd be here when he wake up."

The line was silent a few seconds. "Stoney…I…I hope you realize what you're asking?"

"I know exactly what I'm asking for. You coming over?"

"I'll have to wait till Carmen gets home."

An hour after their talk, Sheila was at the front door. He'd always found her extremely attractive, but today, she beamed radiance.

Her hair was cleverly coiled to form a turban, highlighting her small oval face. Each sensuous curve of her thick body threatened to burst the seams of her thin, summer dress.

"Damn!" Stoney exclaimed. He stepped back for a full view.

"What?"

He whistled. "That dress is definitely sayin'

something."

Sheila blushed.

As she entered the house, Stoney caught wind of her perfume. A soft, leafy scent that was easy to inhale. "You want something to drink?"

"Yes, please. As hot as it is, I should've had you come to my house." She followed Stoney into the kitchen.

"I don't think so. All those Bey-Bey kids running 'round that place?"

"So? And don't be talking about my boops either." She playfully slapped his arm. While he poured two glasses of lemonade, she eased behind him and wrapped her arms around his waist. "I'm glad you called Stoney. I needed to get out of that house for a while."

"And you wanted me to come over there?"

"Oh, stop it. You would've enjoyed the attention."

"Not as much as I would without them around."

It had taken Stoney and Sheila less than an hour to find themselves wrapped in the other's arms, winded after a rugged round of sex. Stoney hadn't thought much about sex since coming home. All his sexual desires had been clouded in his grief. Thankfully, with Sheila, he felt comfortable enough to break through that mold.

"You O.K.?" Sheila asked.

"I'm all right. I'm glad Clara kept Craig's army cot or you might'a crushed Jamal."

"Me?" She laid her head on his broad chest. "You the one that's wild. I know it's been a long time, but dang, I might be walking bowlegged for a month."

"That's O.K., you'll still be my baby - bowlegged and

all."

Stoney had reluctantly broken free of Sheila's grasp to answer a phone call from Big Al. The call had come just short of eleven o'clock, and within the hour, Stoney was entering The Lounge. He spotted Al wobbling toward him with what seemed to be orange juice in a glass. Stoney knew better. The man's beady eyes were bloodshot, and his speech was slurred.

"Stoney, my man. I tol' you I was gonna look out, right?"

"Without a doubt."

"I'm glad you made it down here 'for she weft." He used Stoney's shoulder for support while pointing towards the rear of the bar.

"Who?"

"Her right 'dere in red."

Three underdressed women wearing plenty of makeup were conversating in a booth.

"Who the hell is that?" Stoney challenged.

"One of 'da girls I tol you 'bout. 'Dat's her. I tol' you I was gonna look out, didn't I? And you know what, Stone…" he rambled on, "I think she know where Monny at."

"You think so, huh?"

He pointed a finger at Stoney and put on his serious face. "Aye, I ain't been wrong yet."

Stoney helped Al to the bar then approached the booth Al had pointed to. "Ladies," he greeted, sure to make eye contact with the woman in red.

Her dress was strapless and displayed plenty of cleavage. Her hair was short, near bald, with thin streaks of tan dye to match her bronze skin. She gave Stoney a crack-toothed smile. "And what can we do you for?" she teased.

Stoney patted his pants pocket knowing all hookers respected the dollar bill. "I'm hoping I can speak to you in private."

She eyeballed Stoney from head to toe, dragged from a cigarette she fingered, then blew a smoke plume up at him. "You don't say? And what makes you think we have something to talk about?"

"Me not calling a friend of ours. So how 'bout it?"

The two other women turned concerned eyes to their friend. "You all right, girl?" the smallest asked.

She didn't answer. Instead, she stared coldly at Stoney. "I'll be outside," he informed her.

Stoney watched from the Caddy the prostitute slink from the bar and peer up and down the dark street. She headed east, opposite Stoney, at a hurried gait. He started the car and eased beside her. "Hey!" he yelled.

She dropped her purse and clutched her chest with one hand as if she was having a heart attack. She saw it was Stoney and grimaced. "What the hell is wrong with you!" she spat.

"My bad," he apologized. "I was trying to get your attention." Inside Stoney was laughing a fit.

She stooped and gathered her purse. "Well, you got it!" He pushed open the car door. "Get in."

It wasn't until he'd wheeled the Caddy across Washington Avenue did he ask her her name.

"Sunshine," she managed while nervously peeking through the rear window.

Stoney strangled his laughter. He understood her edginess, having been on the run himself. "Look, Sunshine, I know what happened with Macky. I don't give a fuck about that. I'm trying to find Monty."

"How the hell am I supposed to know where some damned Monty at? I ain't his keeper."

Stoney abruptly pulled the car to the curb and shifted the gear to 'park'. "Relax. I just wanna talk to the brother and I heard you two were together."

She balled her face into a rainbowed mask. "Who tol' you that?"

"That's not important. Do you know where he at? Or do I have to run your ass to Mackey's front door?" He switched the gear back to 'drive'.

"Look, whatever your name is…"

"Stoney."

"Whatever. I left that stingy mutherfucker in Atlantic City early this mornin' and ain't seen him since."

"You think he still there?"

"No."

"Why not?"

"Because…When we was gettin' high, he packed up and said he had to make a drop at Amityville."

"The smokehouse?"

"I don't know anything 'bout no smokehouse. He just said Amityville."

Stoney peeled a ten from his pocket and gave it to her. "Where you wanna get dropped off at?" he asked.

She tucked the money deep into her bra. "Texas."

Amityville stood five-stories, two larger than other

homes on 13th & Webster. The city had declared the building abandoned years ago - and it looked it - tore up from the floor up. At night, Amityville appeared downright spooky. It's only been two years since officials had discovered nine bodies in its ruins. Ever since knowing, residents crossed the street when passing it by. Rumor has it that, within its gory interior and high-weeded yard, numerous corpses still lie buried.

Stoney pulled the car onto the curb, opposite the smoke-house, and grabbed a flashlight from the glove compartment. He dreaded having to traipse through the tall weeds to the building's rear. Fortunately, halfway through the tuft, he spotted a slate of wood, partially covering a small cubby-hole at the building's side. As he neared the cove, a singeing odor forced him to pinch close his nostrils. He pulled the plank from the hole and stepped inside.

Getting around the place was simple. During his days of street dealing, he'd stashed many packages within Amityville's walls. If all remained true, he'd find plenty of coke-smokers on the third, fourth, and fifth floors. He found Monty on the fourth, in a candle-lit room with the heads of two women pushed firmly into his groin. Stoney pulled back the linen sheet covering the entrance. "Enjoying yourself?" Stoney chided, expecting the women to scatter like roaches. Instead, each turned slowly toward him, unashamed.

"Who's that?" Monty replied dully.

Both women stood and halfheartedly covered skeletal bodies with thin arms.

Stoney snatched the sheet from the doorway and tossed it to them.

While the girls wrapped themselves, Monty pulled his pants up from around his ankles, squinted, then smiled. "Stoney?"

"Yeah, it's me. I see you're still into the same old shit."

Stoney cued the women to leave with a nod toward the door and a cold stare.

They didn't hesitate.

"Why'd you do that?" Monty complained.

"Because our business ain't hoe business."

Confused, Monty pulled on his T-shirt. His overly plump lips were twisted sideways. "What business you talking about?"

Stoney stepped closed to his ex-partner. "I need to know who killed my peeps. If anybody know, you do."

Monty was of medium build with a huge head and a crew cut. He shoved his hands in his two-hundred-dollar silk and wool pants pockets, eyed his gator shoes, and shook his head sadly. "Stoney, I swear I ain't heard shit. I tried to find out something. . .but…it's like…like the mutherfucker's vanished."

"Come on, Monty, don't hand me this shit. Don't nothin' go down without you knowing something."

"This did. Whoever did it is keepin' this on the DL."

Stoney left Amityville puzzled. He trusted Monty's word. If Monty hadn't heard anything, chances were, nobody has. Someone knew something…somewhere, Stoney believed. His problem now circled around where to look.

Between the two rectangular, red-clothed tables stood a miked oak podium. Seated at the tables were a wide range of law enforcement officials, including Ryan, all swept by the huge number of concerned African American residents trickling through the recreation center's doors.

The meeting had begun with a seven-minute speech from the city's mayor. The district's councilman's speech followed and so on down the chain of big wigs until Ryan, the last, found himself being introduced to the audience.

Ryan's speech included tip-hotlines, his view on the district's need for additional police protection, and advice for residents needing instruction on how to prevent victimization. At the meeting's conclusion, Ryan felt the debates had gone well. Resident's gripes had been addressed, drug prevention discussed, and the Police Commissioner, through pushy residents' cohesions had volunteered an increase in patrol cars monitoring the area. Ryan left the colloquium high-spirited.

The drive home was a short drive across the Parkway and east on Midvale. After a quick stop for groceries, mostly T.V. dinners, Ryan turned the key in his home's front door and paused. The creases in his forehead dipped, and instinctively, he snatched his .38 revolver from its shoulder holster. He quizzed himself whether he'd forgotten to lock the door. He decided he'd locked it - or, had he? Even as he twisted the doorknob, he questioned himself. Tighter, he gripped the gun as he entered the house. In the home's darkness, only a glimmer from a kitchen light filtered through. His heart raced. This morning when he'd left, he made certain he'd turned was sure of. He crouched with his

.38 and with all the lights off. This he readied slightly above his right shoulder while continuing to ease toward the light. He listened to the quietness. There was nothing. And when he finally reached the kitchen, there was still nothing. He turned toward the stairs. One stair at a time he took. The single stair he recalled that squeaked, he skipped as he headed to an upstairs twice the darkness of downstairs. He no longer had the kitchens glimmer of light to guide him and was forced to click on the hallway light. His bedroom door was closed. He'd left it open. Again, he readied the gun at his shoulder. He braced himself alongside the door, slowly opened it, and hit the light-switch just inside the room. Ryan froze. Deitra - she never budged from her sleep.

Morning arrived to the Pages' bedroom just as most of the night had gone - with glimpses of the couple reuniting with whimpers and whispers of their devotion to one another. Forgotten, for the moments they cuddled, were the grievances and sorrow endured during their separation. Each fought off the temptation to speak in fear of losing the moment to uncertainty.

All day and through the evening the couple ate and made love. And by 11 p.m., both lay entangled, silent and sated. Ryan swallowed to wet his throat and spoke. "I'm glad you're here."

"Me, too," Deitra purred, adjusting her body to his. "You staying?"

She slithered to her side of the bed with a huff. "Do we have to go through this right now?"

"Come on, Dee, I have to know."

"Why, Ryan? Will it make a difference?"

"Of course, it will."

"Until when…the next case?"

He sensed her mood swinging back to the icy barrier that had taken months to thaw. He regretted asking the question. "I promised you things would be different, and 1 meant it."

"I hope so."

For Ryan, sleep wouldn't come easy. From the television to Deitra his eyes darted. Channel 7's account of Councilman Fontes's murder was airing. The anchorman reported that one of the bodyguards murdered had been an undercover federal agent investigating Fontes's dealings. Ryan was near-certain he'd saw the black suspect somewhere before – somewhere recently.

He crept from the bed to the study and phoned the news station. He spoke inquisitively to a Mr. Crosby, the editorial manager. In twenty minutes, Ryan was snatching a black and white printout of Daewoo's image from his fax machine. He compared the fax with the mugshots he'd shown Malissa Gordon.

None matched.

For an hour, he searched through computer files of felons and came up empty. Just as he was about to quit, before Deitra discovered he was missing, he pulled the videotape he'd received from Officer Murrell from the desk draw and scanned it, hoping, unsure if the image he was searching for would appear.

Then it did. Nearly three-quarters of the way through the tape, Daewoo's image appeared. "Bingo." Ryan said triumphantly. He wondered how the puzzle fitted. One moment the suspect is entering one of Philadelphia's most notorious projects then entering a councilman's home. He allowed the tape to run. The times he'd watched the surveillance tape, he'd not paid much attention to the U-turn the man-made in Saigon's lobby. But now, everything about the man was suspicious. Questions began to form in Ryan's mind. What about the kid entering next? Were the two together? Malissa Gordon had said there were two men.

Enriched with confidence, he ejected the tape and returned to bed more invigorated than ever before. He could sense how close the ending was. He was sure he'd pegged his man. He curled himself around Deitra from behind, cupped a breast, and planted a series of small kisses along her nape until she stirred and accepted him into her.

"Deal the fuckin' things, why don't cha?" the skinny, long-nosed man barked. He anted up his twenty-dollar bill.

The dealer placed the deck in front of Frank to be cut. "Straight Poker's the game," he replied while Frank, stone-faced, cut the deck.

Tonight, it was just the three of them: Mickey "The Snout", Morandini, Benji "The Button", Bannelli, and Frank "Fingers" Russo.

For the past twelve years, the back room of "Bannetti's Pawn Shop" has hosted their poker games and, as usual, a thick cloud of cigar smoke hung above their heads. In one corner, a small fridge. An old, brown leather couch, an antique desk, and a well-stocked bar were the room's only other furnishings besides the poker table and chairs.

"So. Whadda you do, Mick?" Frank asked. "You in or out?"

"What do you think? I ain't hadda hand worth playin' all freakin' night." He tossed his cards in. "I fold."

"How 'bout you, Buttons? Two hundred's the bet?"

The pudgy man fingered his cash while he considered it.

"I'll call," he answered, adding two c-notes to the pot.

"Three aces, king high," Frank boasted.

"Shit!" Buttons cursed. He slammed his two pairs to the table, faces down, and stood up frowning. "I'm sorry, fellas, I can't seem to get it goin'. I'ma call it a night. Hell, if I wanted to give my money away, I'd take my mother-in-law shopping." He finished off his double scotch.

"You can't do that!" Frank protested. "It's your game!'

"I don't give a shit. I'm out."

Frank turned to Mickey. "I guess that goes for your skinny, chickenshit ass, too, huh?"

Mickey shrugged. "You too hot for me, Frank."

"Well, ain't that just like you two cocksuckers - scared dead to lose a coupla bucks after cleanin' me out for years. I swear…" Frank scolded. "I gotta wonder 'bout the company I keep. You pricks. Where's the morality?"

At 1 a.m., Frank labored the two-block walk from Bannetti's to his own home. The quiet Society Hill neighborhood gleamed from the earlier rain, and tiny, white specks from a star-filled sky danced in the tarred streets each time a vehicle whizzed by.

The short walk had given Frank time to sober a bit before listening to Daewoo's phone message. Now that he had, he regretted having given Daewoo his home number. He felt bad for Daewoo. He, too, had no idea Fontes would be killed. He'd been double-crossed by his boss as well, and regardless of how he felt about Daewoo or the situation, when "The Boss" says you're history - you're history. He reached for the telephone and sighed.

Ryan finished off the best breakfast he's had in months, refolded his Daily News, and grinned as he listened to Deitra in the living room match the friendliness of two Jehovah's Witnesses." Dee, hon, I have to go," he called to her from the kitchen. "I'll call you later." He heard his wife excuse herself.

When Deitra entered the kitchen, her smile was broad, and she pointed a finger accusingly. "What do you think you're doing?" she asked, catching him at the backdoor.

"Escaping."

"Really. From whom?" His eyes rose above her shoulder toward the living room.

"I'd rather not say."

"You think you so slick, don't you?"

"No."

"Yes, you do."

"No, I don' t."

"Then why not use the front door like a normal person?"

She hoisted onto her toes and kissed his cheek.

"Because I'm not normal."

"I'll vouch for that."

Both stared into the other's eyes.

"Will you be here when I get in?" Ryan asked.

"It's possible." She wrapped her arms around his waist and peered even deeper into his eyes. "I'll tell you what - we'll try the whole family dinner thing tonight, O.K.? If the children feel you've suffered enough, I'll consider staying."

"Oh, you will, huh? I guess I better start sweetening up the judge then." He scooped her small frame even deeper into him and kissed her lovingly.

The drive to the precinct was laggard. As soon as Ryan had arrived, he'd made arraignments to interview Malisa Gordon. He now had a name to match his suspect's face. David Stokes. Ryan again scanned the department's skeletal file on Stokes. One prior arrest for a narcotics sale eighteen months ago. A case unresolved. A warrant for the twenty-eight-year-old was still active. He closed the file again, wondering how someone could graduate so quickly from petty drug dealing to murdering a prominent councilman, a federal agent, bodyguards, and an old couple. Then again, he conceded, he'd never underestimate the lengths an addict would go to feed his habit, whether his addition was drugs, money, power, or sex.

With time to spare before visiting the hospital, Ryan fought to clear most of the paperwork from his desk before sauntering into the captain's office.

Plummer looked up from his desk. "What is it, Ryan?"

"I need a minute." He carefully closed the door. "First of all, sir, here's the Thorne report you asked for." He pushed a scrawny folder at the man.

Plummer gripped the folder and dropped it to the

desk. "And second?"

"Secondly, I believe I'll be finishing up on the Montross case soon."

"That's great. Wrap it up and put your report on my desk," he replied dismissively.

"I'll need your help, though."

"What is it?"

"I need a warrant issued on this guy." Ryan passed him the Stokes file.

Plummer scanned the file and shrugged. "So, what do you need me for?"

"Because he's also a suspect in the Fontes case."

Interest sprung to Plummer's face. He rifled through the file once more while Ryan continued speaking.

"And if I'm right…no sooner he's picked up the feds will be pulling him outta here."

"So, we'll get 'em when they're done."

"That's exactly it," Ryan pointed out. "I need him for questioning now. If the feds get him, I can forget it. He may never turn on his accomplice. There'll be nothing to gain."

Plummer folded his pudgy hands on the desk. "Again, what do you need from me?"

Ryan explained.

Afterward, Plummer sat mulling over the situation. "I see your point, Ryan. Unfortunately, I'm obligated to report an arrest if the feds come snooping; however, because you're in my pocket for a favor, I'll prolong the situation as long as possible. Will that do?"

"That's all I ask, sir. It may not even be necessary."

At 9:30 a.m., Ryan was at Malissa Gordon's bedside.

He'd stopped at the hospital's gift shop and purchased a small, pink teddy-bear wearing an apron that read: *"SQUEEZE ME SOMETHING AWFUL."* When he'd given the gift to Malissa, she'd rewarded him with a tight smile and a curt thank you.

She looks as if she hadn't lost any more weight since he'd visited last. Her dark eyes were still terribly hollow, her head bore a fresh, gauze turban, and her skin was as chafe as a crocodile's.

"Good morning, everyone," Doctor Hughes beamed from behind a portable twenty-inch television/VCR she was wheeling into the room. She plugged the television into a wall outlet then stood on the opposite side of the bed. "I hope this is satisfactory, Detective."

"It's fine."

Ryan had preset the surveillance tape. Seconds into it, he watched Malissa's eyes widen when Daewoo's image appeared entering Saigon. Ryan crouched beside her. "Take your time, Malissa. Take a good look at him. Give it a second…another…there." He quickly freeze-framed Daewoo facing the camera.

Malissa watched silently for a few seconds, then nodded. "All right. That's good. You're doing well," Ryan coaxed.

"His name's not Quawee like you thought. His file says his nickname's Daewoo. Could Daewoo be the name you heard the other man call him?"

"Probably," she replied hoarsely.

"That's fine. We'll come back to that later." He looked to the doctor who gave an O.K. to continue. "Here we go," he began again, repeating the process, only this time pausing the tape on the second man. He turned back to Malissa.

Her eyes seemed as if they would burst from their sockets. Her bony fingers covered most of her gasp, but still a muffled, "Oh my, God!" escaped her.

She was frightened and both Ryan and Doctor Hughes saw it. "O.K., Detective Page, I think that's enough," the doctor interrupted. "It doesn't take much more to recognize that they're the ones. Now, if you don't mind…"

Ryan ejected the cassette. "Malissa, I'm sorry to have taken you through this. Are you all right?"

She didn't answer. She continued to stare at the blank screen.

Ryan assumed she was reliving the horror she'd endured. He left the hospital feeling numb.

Ryan, two uniformed officers, and an Assistant District Attorney, sat long-faced in the squad room after returning empty-handed from what was supposed to be a routine arrest.

In just an hour after leaving the hospital, Ryan had formulated the team to arrest Daewoo. The plan had been simple. But no one had anticipated the F.B.I. having already trashed David Stokes's home.

"I don't believe this crap!" Ryan stormed. He slammed a folder on the metal desktop.

"Well, get used to it," said the A.D.A., repeatedly slapping a palm with a rolled file.

"I know one damn thing…" Ryan said matter of fact. "They better catch this fucker before I do because I'm not giving his ass up till it's raw."

The larger of the two uniformed cops patted Ryan on the back. "Well, it was a good try. If you need me, holler."

"That goes for me as well," the A.D.A. added.

The three men filtered from the squad room, leaving Ryan cursing the F.B.I. for basically shitting on his badge by over- looking tris. investigation. He flopped into his desk chair and tried focusing on the Asian suspect Malissa had identified as the shooter.

Chapter Eight

Since 8 a.m., two police officers draped in flak-jackets and black khakis tucked in black leather boots, have been stationed on the roof of a two-story brownstone across the street from "Little Italy." At street level, another two officers, both trying to look as inconspicuous as possible in street clothes, covered the north and south corners of the street while a third team of two detectives sat placidly in a grey Skylark parked half a block away from the bar's entrance.

All this Daewoo witnessed from the ruins of an abandoned home a few houses away. His instincts were right not to trust Frank to meet him. With his anger rising and his fears confirmed, Daewoo hurriedly stumbled through the rubble and out onto the street, opposite the police stakeout.

He walked the smaller, less frequented streets, cursing his stupidity, piecing together the scenario. He even pictured Frank and the Serragucchies laughing over a brew, joking about how dumb a moolie they had suckered. Disgusted, he turned onto a main street, still cussing, desperately needing a cigarette.

Wawa's bustle of business hadn't yet begun. The aisles were empty of customers and, the two female employees, garbed in maroon and tan striped uniforms, took their stations when Daewoo entered the store.

While the employees busied themselves, Daewoo roamed the aisles, undecided, paranoid that both women's eyes were locked onto his back, wondering if they recognized him from last night's news report. He quickly microwaved an egg & cheese omelet and purchased a pack of Newport. As he was leaving, he noticed the newspapers stacked on each side of the entrance.

Normally, he'd have passed them by, but the bold, black headline of the Philadelphia Daily News read: "STATE COUNCILMAN SLAIN!" and beneath in small caption: "Suspects sought - story on page 4." There was also a quarter page photo of Fontes's estate, and a blurred copy of the photo Channel 7 had aired of Daewoo and Mario entering the property. Daewoo snatched a paper from the pile and flipped to page 4. He read for a moment, trying to find mention of the Serragucchies.

There was none.

"Excuse me, sir," said the cashier.

Daewoo spun around with confused eyes. "What?"

"I'm sorry, sir, that's not allowed. If you want to read a paper, you'll have to buy one."

He fished three quarters from his pocket and dropped them on the counter.

For a third time, Daewoo read the article, hoping the wording would change and that somehow, someone had misprinted what he'd supposedly done.

The article read that Councilman Fontes had been under federal investigation for illegal campaign contributions, racketeering, and money laundering. It also exposed Daewoo as Fontes's source of narcotics and that several of Fontes's closest associates claim that he owed an enormous gambling debt to the mob. What Daewoo found even more disturbing was that one of the slain bodyguards was an F.B.I. mole.

Daewoo crumbled the newspaper and stuffed it into a nearby trash can. "What the fuck is goin' on?" he whispered as he plodded toward 13th Street wondering how he, suddenly, kept getting involved in homicides. He needed time to think.

Every image his mind could conjure was of him being sacrificed, nailed to a cross with the word "murderer" burned into his forehead. He gripped the Wawa bag tighter and quickly covered the five blocks to Scorpio's, hoping he'd figure out what to do after he'd rested.

The small room at Scorpio's was clammy and reeked of urine. "Twenty dollars for this shit?" Daewoo grumbled to himself. He tossed his bagged breakfast onto a jagged dresser.

A twin bed, a dresser, and a large wicker-chair crowded the place. A dingy, beige shade covering a single window gave the room a sallow glow. Daewoo was surprised the bed had been made - with clean sheets - at least they appeared clean. He pulled the wad of bills from his pocket and dropped it onto the bed. "Setup money," he said knowingly. "I should just call the cops." He laughed at the idea. He'd no way of proving he knew the Serragucchies - or Frank, for that matter. He was certain wearing a wire would be useless. No way, he believed, would Frank allow him anywhere near him after this mess.

He pulled four baggies of cocaine from his pocket; cocaine he'd bought from Beasty to ease any suspicions she may have about him renting a room. He stared at the packets in his palm then replaced them along with the money. He knew getting high would be suicide and that he'd need to be clear-headed in order to survive.

Exhausted, he stretched out across the bed and allowed his eyelids to close. Trina would probably hate him after this, he thought. He pictured her holding his son on her lap engrossed in a fierce interview with the police. He realized she'd probably tell them all about his great new job.

Because of his fretful night's sleep, Stoney sat along the edge of the bed, massaging tired eyes, hoping to erase the cruel images that had invaded his dream, a heart-wrenching, surreal dream filled with vivid, grotesque images of his mother and Paul's bullet ridden bodies.

Behind him, Sheila lay asleep on her back, and on her chest, Jamal lay content, staring curiously at his father while sucking ferociously on two tiny fingers.

"Aye little man," Stoney said wearily, prying the child from his mother. "What flavor are those?" He tugged the boy's fingers from his mouth.

At twenty-one months, the child had already cleared forty pounds and was racing toward three feet in height. When a stout, pinching odor seeped into Stoney's nostrils, he peeked inside the child's pamper then to the sardonic grin on the boy's face. Stoney smiled.

Two hours later, after Jamal had been fed, cleaned,

and laid to nap, Sheila and Stoney shared a bacon & egg breakfast and cuddled in the quietness, idling as the television stared back at the two. The telephone's jingling separated them.

Stoney lifted the receiver on the second ring. Before answering, he admired Sheila's nakedness saunter across the room. Only when she'd pulled on a robe did he speak to the caller. It was Frank Russo.

"You see the news yet?" Frank asked."

"No."

"Turn to Channel 7."

Stoney did so. "Yeah, I got it. What's happening?"

"Just wait a second," Frank replied.

Both ends of the line were quiet while the Asian anchor woman told the story.

"Our Channel 7 news stations have received new information today from the Philadelphia Police Department. One of the two men sought in the brutal slayings of Councilman Miquel Fontes and his three bodyguards, one of which was discovered to be a federal officer, is also wanted for questioning in connection with a double homicide and near-fatal shooting that had occurred two months ago at the Martin Luther King Project. One of the men, sought for questioning, is David Stokes, a twenty-eight-year-old, black male, who also resides in the project. A photo of Daewoo was aired over the right shoulder of the anchor-woman as she continued. "It has also been reported that a second suspect is being sought in connection with the Montross' murders. His name is still unknown, but authorities have released this footage of the suspects…"

The video of Daewoo and Tone entering Saigon was shown. The anchorwoman concluded with the number of a tip-hotline and the mention of a sizeable reward.

"Stoney, you there?" Frank asked.

Stoney swallowed to rid the dryness in his throat. "Yeah. I'm still here."

"For what it's worth, Stoney, I know one of the cockroaches that did this."

Stoney was stunned silent. He'd recognized Daewoo immediately and was shocked he'd have anything to do with the killings. Nevertheless, an intense rage had begun within him.

"Listen, Stoney. I want you to use your head in dealing with this thing."

"I hear you," Stoney muttered.

"Good. I tell you what - you come pass the club later - we'll put somethin' together."

"Sure."

That cigar cloud gripped the low ceiling of Little Italy, creating a suffocating staleness throughout the bar. The few attending regulars, stoned in their red, vinyl booths, squinted each time the front door opened, and sunlight invaded their dim sanctuary.

"So. You sure you all right?" Frank asked for the third time.

Stoney frowned. "Come on, Frank, with the bullshit. How many times you gonna ask me that?"

"I just want you to know that you can count on me." The two were seated in Frank's usual booth.

"How about loaning me a piece?" Stoney asked.

"Something clean and untraceable."

With displeasure, Frank pulled the wireframes from his face, stirred, then rubbed a freckled hand down his mug. "A piece, huh?"

"Yeah. I prefer automatics."

"That I can do."

"How long I gotta wait?"

"After Friday."

"What's the hold up?"

"It ain't like I carry that kinda shit in my trunk. I gotta"

"Cut the bullshit, Frank," Stoney interrupted. "You and I both know if you wanted a fuckin' SCUD missile, that shit'll be out front in an hour."

Frank smiled, replaced his glasses and settled into his seat. "You're right. I definitely can get it sooner. But I got my reasons." As if confiding a secret, Frank leaned forward and whispered. "Look at the whole picture, Stoney. This guy's gonna get nabbed. For Christ's sake, he killed a fed and a councilman - a crime that's already gotten national attention and the F.B.I. on his tail. If that ain't enough, he got the locals chasin' his ass for double-homicide. This guy's hot, Stoney, and it's only a matter of time before they catch 'em." Frank paused to finish his drink.

Stoney leaned back, content on hearing Frank out.

"This is how I see it - I give you a piece - You run around tryin' to pop the guy - next thing you know, you're back in the joint - somethin' I'd hate to see happen."

"So, what am I supposed to do?"

"Lay low. Be smart and let the feds do their job. When

they catch 'em, then step to the plate. I ain't never seen the feds not find somebody they really wanted. There's always some greedy fuck waitin' to collect the reward."

Stoney watched the man closely. He knew Frank Russo did no favors for free. He decided to bite. "O.K., I'll wait. But I still want the piece - just in case."

Relief settled across Frank's face. "Good. And now, I need a favor.'

"I knew it was too good to be true. What kind?"

"The usual job. But I need it done Friday."

"Does it pay?"

"I always pay."

"Then I'm in."

Amidst the bedroom's muss of strewn clothing and gloom, Stacey idled in front of her 13-inch, color television confused and awaiting the 6 p.m. news broadcast.

She'd already bitten away what little fingernails she'd grown and was now chewing on the skin of one thumb. She sat compelled to watch, yet another telecast in hopes that the media's heinous lies have changed about her man. She questioned her own sanity, her reasons for loving a man who'd abused her.

She'd always classified herself as one of the new breed of independent women. And yet, in some twisted, tainted way, she welcomed Tone's hold over her.

She stopped biting her thumb to adjust thin hair rollers when the knock came at her bedroom door.

"Stacey, come out here," her mother called.

Stacey sucked her teeth, swore, then peeked an irritated expression from her bedroom door. "For what?"

"Someone's here to talk to you."

In a rush not to miss the news broadcast, she hurriedly pulled on a floral housecoat, passed down from her mother, and entered the living room. She stared curiously at the tall, bearded man standing next to her mother.

Ryan flashed the girl his badge. "Stacey, my name is Detective Ryan Page."

Stacey pulled the housecoat tighter around her and cast a wondering look to her mother.

"Would you mind if I ask you a few questions?" Ryan asked.

"About what?"

Ryan smiled. "Don't worry, you're in no trouble. I just need some information about your boyfriend."

"I don't have a boyfriend." Her tone was defiant, and her eyes darted in her mother's direction.

Ryan picked up on the girl's fear of her mother knowing. "Well, maybe he's not your boyfriend," he conceded. "Our information isn't always right. Sometimes it takes months to straighten out what someone's told us." With a light laugh, he pulled photos of Tone and Daewoo from his inside blazer pocket. "Do you recognize any of these guys?"

She held the photos with both hands. "No," she lied, surprised at how easily the lie had slipped from her lips. Her expression was even as she returned the pictures.

"Are you sure, Stacey?"

"Yes, I'm sure. What makes you think I know them anyway?"

"Someone gave us your name. They said you and this guy, Tone, hang out together."

"They lied."

Ryan pocketed the photos. "Stacey, how old are you?"

"Sixteen."

Ryan gestured to the sofa. "Have a seat for a minute." He turned to the girl's mother. "Is it all right with you, Mrs. Baker?"

"Sure. Have a seat, Detective."

Reluctantly, Stacey slumped to the sofa with folded arms. "Stacey, listen," Ryan said. "I know you believe you're doing the right thing by covering for this guy…"

"I ain't."

"Hold it. Hear me out." When she settled back down, he continued. "I don't want you to feel like I'm dumping on you. I just don't think you fully understand how dangerous your boy… well - this guy is."

"I told you I don't know him!" she spat. Her eyes were small balls of fire. She wished the cop would just leave her alone so that she could go back to her television. She needed to speak with Tone and ask him why everyone was telling these lies. She was sure he'd never do something so awful.

As if he'd heard her plea, Ryan frowned and stood up. He offered the girl his card.

"Does this mean we're done?" she asked.

"Not unless there's something you'd like to tell me."

"No."

"Then, I guess we are."

In one swoop Stacey snatched the card and stormed back to her bedroom.

Ryan turned to the teenager's mother, who in turn gave the detective a shrug.

At 4 p.m., Daewoo awoke groggy and fully clothed. Chill bumps from the room's dampness, covered him, and the stench of urine seemed to have magnified while he'd slept. He wiped at his nose and stared at the beige, yellow-stained ceiling. Out of habit, he grabbed at his pockets. He was relieved no one crept in the room with a razor during his sleep and slashed his pockets.

The bathroom was as tormenting as his room. After splashing cold water on his face, he lumbered downstairs into a swarm of alcoholics having assembled in full force - some still familiar from yesterday when he'd first arrived. From eighteen to elderly, they packed the tiny living room sipping from a cup, can, or bottle.

"Watch it now!" a huge chocolate woman screamed while doing The Bump to the remix of Janet Jackson's "That's the Way Love Goes."

Daewoo weaved through the gyrating bodies toward the front door. With three steps to go, a hand grabbed him.

"Where the hell you been?" Tone asked.

Daewoo stopped mid-stride. He glared down at the eighteen-year-old slouched on the dirty, green sofa. Tone's eyes resembled coin slots and his speech was slurred. "Where

I been? Where you been is the question," retorted Daewoo.

"You see me. I'm chillin'." Tone hoisted himself from the sofa and stumbled toward the stairs. He gestured for Daewoo to follow.

Once upstairs, Tone led Daewoo to a room slightly larger than the room Daewoo had rented. The furnishings were exact.

Daewoo sniffed the air. There was no odor. "So. What's up?"

Tone took a seat in the wicker chair. "You tell me. I don't believe you this close to the jets - 'specially the way 5 oh ridin'."

Daewoo closed the door and sat on the bed. "You know I ain't do that shit, right?"

Tone shrugged. "I don't give a fuck if you did or didn't. All I know is - if I was your ass - I'd get ghost in a hurry." Tone pulled a blunt from his sweatpants pocket and lit it.

"Do me a favor, Tone?"

He choked back the Blunt's smoke. "What?"

"Call my girl for me?"

"From where? Ain't no phone here."

"Use a phone booth then."

"I don't think so, my man." Tone plucked the blunt ash to the floor before passing it to Daewoo.

"Don't tell me you done did somethin' else?"

"It ain't that. I guess you ain't watched the news, huh?"

"No. Why?"

"They got us on the Most Wanted List for that shit in

Saigon."

Daewoo pulled the blunt from his lips. "I know you lyin'!" he snapped. He stood and paced the floor, cursing in breaths of fury. His arms flailed wildly and his facial expressions suggested he might burst into tears at any second. He turned his back to Tone and stood silent, suppressing every instinct to bash Tone's face in. It was Tone's fault, he believed. Tone's murders he was being accused of. He gathered himself and stared at the teenager. "What did they say?"

"That we're suspects and they wanna question us."

"Fuck that! I don't know shit about nothin'!" Daewoo spat.

He handed the blunt back to Tone.

"That's what I was hopin' you'd say."

For Daewoo, night had arrived slowly. While awaiting the shelter of darkness, he'd come up with a plan and had already begun executing it. It had taken him twenty minutes to slither through alleys to Tortelli's Pawn Shop and purchase a mini camcorder. Within minutes of returning, he'd set the second phase of his plan in motion. The rest depended on Tone, and him having already smoked himself comatose helped as well.

Daewoo peered down at the snoring teenager then to the wicker chair, concealing the Phillies cap concealing the camera. It'd taken four shakes to rouse Tone from his sleep, and now that he'd awakened, Daewoo's heartbeat raced.

"What time is it?" Tone grumbled.

"Time to get up."

"Get up for what?"

Daewoo sat in the wicker chair across from the bed, careful not to block the camera's eye. "You know better than me that no soon as one of those drunks downstairs recognize us, our asses is out."

"Stop being paranoid all the time. You niggas fuck me up wit' that crybaby shit. Y'all be out here takin' marks off, and no sooner you catch a case, y'all start bitchin' instead 'a suckin' it the fuck up."

Daewoo ceased his chance to bring up the killings. "I ain't got no problem accepting shit J do, but you the one killed Candy and her ol' man."

"So the fuck what?" Tone admitted. "You seen that bitch spit in my face."

"Yeah, I saw it. But now you got me caught up in the bullshit."

"I ain't got you caught up in shit. You could 'a rolled if you wanted to."

"And got shot?"

Behind Daewoo, the camera recorded their conversation.

Daewoo was confident he'd enough on tape and decided to not push his luck. He pulled the four bags of coke, he'd purchased earlier, from his pocket. "You still get down?" he asked.

Tone shrugged, still heated from their conversation. "So - so"

Daewoo tossed over the bags. "If you get some tools, you can go 'head and get down."

Tone scooped the packets from the bed without a thank you and left the room.

Quickly Daewoo pulled the tape from the camera and stuffed it in his waistband. The camera he hid in the bottom dresser drawer until later.

When Tone returned, Daewoo was back in the wicker chair with his legs crossed and a wide smile.

"What the hell you smilin' 'bout?" Tone asked.

"Don't pay me no mind," Daewoo mused. "I'm trippin'. I think I just figured out a way to get both of us enough dough to disappear."

Chapter Nine

A paucity of long, milky clouds etched themselves into a pavonine sky, and a delightfully sweet breeze carried small strips of debris across the blacktop of the project courtyard. In front of one rowhome was Milton Hightower's Caddy. In it, Stoney watched his father exit the house. He'd until 8 p.m. to collect the truck, along with an unknown partner, for a delivery in Marion County.

The Caddy dipped sideways when Milton Hightower slid his near-four-hundred-pound frame behind the wheel. Somber lines covered his face, and, for two blocks, they rode in silence.

"What's this job Clara's been telling me about?" Milton asked.

"Just a truckin' gig."

"Are they paying good money?"

"Enough.'

"No amount's ever enough."

"Let's just say it's enough to make you an offer for this baby here." Stoney slid his hand across the car's wooden dash.

"Ha! You wish. You know how many pennies I saved to get this car? Three years' worth. When this sucker go to the grave, I'll be in it."

Stoney's face became taunt and serious.

"Ay, man, I'm sorry," his father apologized. "I didn't mean to stir things up again."

"1 know."

"Do you know the guys they say did it?"

"Just one of 'em."

Milton eyed his son. "You've been downtown looking for them, haven't you?"

"Not really."

"Not really, huh? Then what's this?" From beneath the driver's seat, Milton produced a 9mm handgun.

"Where'd you get that?"

"You know damn well where it came from. In my house." He slid the gun across the seat to Stoney, who stuffed it into his waistband. "You know if they find that gun on you, you're going back to jail, right?"

"Come on, Pop, I'm not for the lecturing. First of all, I didn't have it on me. Second, why'd you go through my closet?"

"Because I pay the bills and Clara does the laundry." Milton breathed deeply. "Stoney, you're a grown man and there ain't much I can tell you. I don't give a shit about that gun being in the house, but I do care whether you're out here or in jail."

The truck depot was a five-story, 1940's red-brick with a four-foot concrete platform running its length. Eight rows of four-by-fours, six-by-sixes, U-Haul's, and pickup-trucks were parked, accepting their cargos from forklifts and laborers.

Stoney had visited the depot twice before his stint in prison and had little problem locating the dispatcher's booth.

"You got papers?" the dispatcher asked. He was an ancient man, whose hands trembled when he accepted Stoney's credentials. Just as shakily, he made a call then returned Stoney's papers along with a set of keys. "81B," he said.

The truck was a four-wheel, reddish-brown heap with a huge logo on its side that read:

GORDON FURNITURE, INC. 47 ABINGTON AVENUE SUSSEX, NJ. 05906

Stoney checked his watch. Seven-forty-five.

Fifteen minutes to meet his partner at the coffee shop across the street, and with ten minutes to spare, he pulled the truck in front of the cafe and beeped the horn four times as planned.

Through the passenger-side window, Stoney observed a man in sweat-gear exit the cafe sipping from a Styrofoam cup. A black Sixers cap concealed the upper portion of the man's face. At thirty-five feet, his pace quickened - thirty feet - twenty-five feet - the Styrofoam cup still raised to his lips and the cap hiding all but the man's eyes.

Something was wrong.

It was the cup, Stoney thought. It never moved.

Stoney gripped the butt of the 9mm tucked in his waistband. He placed the automatic on his lap and braced himself.

At fifteen feet, the cup still lingered. Stoney locked onto his target. At ten feet, he knew. It was the guy's eyes that alerted him. Young, menacing eyes. Eyes with a history as far back as the evening news. Eyes that screamed trouble. Stoney raised the gun. As quick as Stoney was to raise his weapon, the driver's side door flew open even quicker and a huge, black .357 magnum pointed him dead. From the barrel to the bearer, Stoney's eyes swept, his gun still pointed toward the passenger side door. Common sense told him he'd lost. Reluctantly, he lowered his gun.

In just seconds, the two hijackers boarded the truck. While the younger of the two frisked him, Stoney bit deep into his bottom lip until the taste of blood and revenge filled his mouth.

Washington Avenue, South Philadelphia's industrial belt, stretched from the Delaware River to Grays Ferry and beyond. A host of factories and massive warehouses lined the avenue's sidewalks, and inside one of the many abandoned warehouses, Daewoo watched as Stoney glared at him in a temper.

"Stoney, it ain't about you."

Daewoo said, having not counted on Stoney being the truck's driver.

Twice on Friday nights, he'd visited the depot and had picked up the exact truck. He'd hoped the routine hadn't changed - and it hadn't.

"I'll tell you one thing…" Stoney threatened, "Your coffins are already made."

"You better worry 'bout your damn self," Tone

replied before dropping seven kilos to the floor. He gallantly adjusted Stoney's confiscated 9mm. in his waistband.

Daewoo stood silent while Tone tied Stoney's wrists and ankles with wire-rope. When the teen was done, Daewoo pulled him aside. "Listen. You remember the deal, right?"

"Yeah, I remember…ten thou' and two bricks."

"And no killing," Daewoo added.

"Man, ain't nobody thinkin' 'bout killin' nobody."

"Good, because shit already hectic enough." Daewoo scanned the darkening room.

The flat was spacious with high ceilings and a narrow hallway prized with a shoddy strip of rust-colored carpeting. The walls were emerald-green. And centered along the largest wall, five massive windows were sectioned in cubes of twelves.

"I'ma check out the rest of the place," Daewoo informed Tone.

Daewoo returned to find Stoney and Tone seated opposite one another. Stoney's mouth had been gagged with a handkerchief, and Tone had already torn into a kilo of cocaine. "The place is empty." Daewoo looked from Tone to Stoney then back to his partner. "What's up with the gag?" he asked.

"He talk too fuckin' much," Tone answered without looking up from the package.

Daewoo wondered if he'd made the right decision to bring Tone along. He decided he had; not only did his plan need a second person, but he needed a cellphone and weapons, things Tone had underground connections to. "Here. I found this in the truck." Daewoo handed Tone a flashlight.

"How much you chargin' this chump for this coke?" Tone asked.

"Twenty thousand." "That's it?"

"I ain't tryin'a be greedy. I just wanna tape his ass. Fuck the money."

Tone stuffed his face into the kilo and snorted. He let loose a fit of coughs then looked up at Daewoo powder-faced, with glazed eyes and a smile. "I always wanted to do that," he bragged.

Daewoo shook his head, bewildered. "See, that's the difference between us. I'm not willin' to kill myself about no drugs."

"You right," Tone agreed, "'cause if I want somethin', I take it and mutherfuck the consequences."

Daewoo saw the wildness in Tone's eyes he'd witnessed in Saigon and tensed with nervousness. The sooner he'd distance himself from the teenager, he thought, the better off he'd be. He pulled the cellphone from his pocket and dialed Frank's number. After four rings, Frank was on the line.

"Where are you?" Frank asked.

"Around."

"Around? What kind of answer is that? I thought you wanted to meet?"

"Come on, Frank, be for real. I know you dropped dime about the meet. I was there. I saw the cops waitin'."

"What's this?" Frank snapped. "If you called to break my balls, your ass is way outta line."

"I'm outta line?" Daewoo countered. "You set me up

and I'm the one outta line, huh? Yeah, well, I suggest you count your drops, Frank. You're short one."

The line was silent.

Daewoo pictured Frank red-faced on the other end. "You moolie mutherfucker!" Frank spat.

Daewoo smiled. After assuring Frank that he'd practically give the cocaine to the Puerto Ricans on spite, Frank agreed to Daewoo's terms. Twenty thousand - *on delivery* - in the morning.

Two hours past. A limber moonlight beamed through the massive windows, providing the warehouse with sufficient light. On the floor with his head reclined against the wall and the open kilo between his legs, sat Tone. He was ripped.

Daewoo looked on, wondering if the teen has a death wish. Each time Tone had risen to pace the shadows of the semi-dark flat, Daewoo had found himself nervously fingering the trigger of the .357. He turned his attention to Stoney, who was bound and gagged, sitting at the far corner of the room. He approached Stoney cautiously, his gun gripped firmly. He untied the gag.

"You all right?" he asked.

Stoney stared with cold, penetrating eyes.

"Hey, I told you this ain't got nothin' to do with you. You just happen to be drivin' the wrong truck. I didn't even know you fuck with that snake."

"Then untie me," Stoney said stiffly.

"I can't do that."

"Why? It ain't about me, remember?"

"You'd probably try and kill me if I did. But you know

what… tomorrow, this whole thing will be straight."

"I guess I suppose to just forget about this, huh?"

Daewoo tucked the gun in his waistband, took a knee, and frustratingly wiped a palm across his face. "Look, Stoney, I know what you're thinkin'. We ain't gotta fake it." He looked to Tone then back to Stoney. "It wasn't me. I'm sorry about what happened to your mom, but I didn't do it. It ain't my make up. I play con and sell slum."

"Don't forget kidnapping," Stoney offered.

Uneasiness settled on Daewoo's face. "I'm sorry about the ropes and shit, but how can I trust you to believe me? I know if the situation was reversed, you'd feel the same way."

The sound of Tone approaching interrupted them.

When Tone arrived, one hand palmed the kilo and in the other hand, the 9mm. Tone stood over them, sweating an ocean and crystal eyed. "Where's the phone?" he murmured.

Daewoo handed him the cellphone. "Who you callin'?"

"My girl."

Rested, Stacey's spirits were high, and her confidence restored in her man. Immediately after Tone had phoned, she'd rushed to her closet and had chosen only her favorite outfits to be taken with her.

From her dresser, she'd plucked up perfumes, cosmetics, jewelry, and from the corner of a mirror, a wallet-size photo of her nephew.

Tone had given her no indication where they'd be going, but for Stacey, just knowing they'd be going together was sufficient.

Shortly after midnight, she'd received his call. "It's me, baby," he'd announced.

"Where are you?" she'd asked.

"Don't worry 'bout that. I'm cool."

"You don't sound the same."

His voice was soft and muffled, effects from the large amount of cocaine he'd snorted. "I got a cold."

She pressed the receiver tighter to her ear. "Tone, what's up with all this stuff they saying?"

"Don't tell me you believe it? They lyin'."

Stacey's eyes swelled with tears. For two days she'd waited to hear her man's side of the story. "I knew it!" she cried. "I knew they were lying."

"Don't they always? Stacey, I called to say I'm sorry 'bout what happened and that I'm 'bout ready to get ghost for a while."

"Why? You didn't do it, right?"

"That's not the point. To them, it doesn't matter."

Stacey had paced to the window and peeked down onto a rare deserted street. "I wanna go with you," she'd said.

"I was hopin' you did."

It was now 6:30 a.m., and with her Gucci bag stuffed and ready, Stacey spun in the mirror, approving her outfit. A thin, black and blue rugby shirt and denims. At her bedroom entrance, she paused to tape an enveloped letter, addressed to her mother, to the door.

Outside, the morning was cool. The sun's warmth hadn't yet reached its peak and not a cloud could be seen across a blue sky.

Stacey chartered one of three neighborhood hacks, a scraggly old man whom she knew cherished his large tan station-wagon. To her delight, the ride had been quick - fifteen minutes at most. Five bucks she paid the driver before stepping onto Washington Avenue, where Tone had agreed to meet her.

The Avenue was empty of pedestrians. A stream of cargo trucks and noisy eighteen-wheelers continuously whizzed by her carrying their own unique sounds. To pass the time, she closed her eyes and tried guessing the types of trucks that drove by her. Not long after she'd begun her game, she opened her eyes and saw Tone a city block's distance, stepping at a feverish pace. He looked down as he walked, his hands hidden within the pockets of his sweatpants.

Stacey gripped the straps of her backpack and hurried towards him. When they embraced, all her fears of him leaving her vanished. She laid her head on his shoulder and exhaled, unaware of the dark blue sedan and white Pontiac that cruised by.

Frank Russo stood on his Townhouse balcony, flaming mad. He'd just finished barking last-minute orders to four mafia soldiers handpicked to help recover the highjacked shipment of cocaine.

"Fuckin' morons. The whole lot of 'em," Frank cursed, handing his morning scotch to a pigeon-faced man at his side. "You tell me how this fuckin' moolie, of all people, just walks in and takes seven keys of stuff? Explain that to me, will ya'?"

"They say it was one of your own people who picked up the truck."

"One of my people, my ass." Frank entered the house. "What about Bernie? Where the fuck was that prick?"

"In the john, tied and gagged."

"That figures. Remind me to fire that no good fuck."

"Sure thing, boss."

Frank's eyes were weary. After receiving Daewoo's call, he'd stalked to his wall safe and ran a shaky finger down his three pages of coded clients. After six calls, he'd tracked which shipment had been clipped and had spent the earlier part of the morning gathering guns, soldiers, and a tactful plan of retribution. He decided to surround the drop with armed men and prevent anyone from leaving the area unnoticed. He'd also stressed to his men the importance of not shooting until after the cocaine had been recovered.

With his plan set, Frank snatched the manila envelope containing the twenty thousand from the foyer table and headed down to the car with the pigeon-faced henchman close behind.

"We should get there in plenty time, boss."

"Yeah, I know. It should give me time to figure out what to do with this prick's corpse."

Chapter Ten

When morning arrived, wooden two-by-fours, iron crates, and plastic bread racks lay scattered throughout the alleyway leading to the courtyard at the warehouse's rear.

Daewoo hoped his ploy would unsettle and force Frank to walk to and from the drop and eliminate what securities a car would provide.

In the courtyard, an aluminum shed hid the highjacked truck. Twenty feet in front of the shed, Daewoo had fixated two kilos atop a stack of overturned bread racks. He figured the makeshift podium would be an ideal place for Frank to give his confession from.

The getaway wasn't as simple. It was chancy and charted tremendous dangers for someone intimidated by heights.

During the night, he'd located a stairway leading to the warehouse's roof. Extending from the roof was a drainpipe he'd shimmy down onto the street. He'd cursed the building's architecture, wondering who'd build a building so large with all its windows on its upper floors. He'd also dreaded each new complication that arose: Tone's unwillingness to stop snorting cocaine and Stacey showing up with wet eyes and insults. There was little Daewoo could do about Stacey. She would be Tone's problem. But he was certain Frank's goons would storm the warehouse immediately after the exchange and warned both teenagers.

"So what?" Tone replied. "So, let the girl meet you somewhere else," Daewoo retorted. The two stood in the courtyard's center, eye to eye. Daewoo's eyes questioning, Tone's motionless, yet, as threatening as an open-mouthed python.

"Let me worry 'bout my girl."

"Whatever."

A half-hour later Daewoo entered the crippled shed and started the videotape. He double-checked the camera's operation light, making sure it was on, covered all but the lens with soiled rags and aimed it toward the bread rack podium. He hustled toward his third-floor watch post overlooking Washington Avenue.

"When's this thing gonna happen?"

Daewoo spun at the sound of Tone's voice. "You stay creepin', don't you?"

"Every chance I get. What's up with the doe?" Believe me, it'll be here." Daewoo returned a watchful eye to the street.

Tone joined him.

"Where's Stacey?" Daewoo asked.

"I gave her the two keys and told 'er to meet me later."

A slight smile crept to Daewoo's face and he nodded

his approval. As an afterthought he looked to Tone. "Why'd you stick around? You got the two keys you wanted."

A look of dejection crossed Tone's face. "I don't believe you even asked me that. For the cash, my man. Why else?"

"That's what I don't understand. You coulda just brodied all the coke and been set."

"That ain't how I roll, D. We in this shit together like I said from the get-go."

The shiny black Lincoln crawled to a stop at the mouth of the alleyway. Frank Rosso, draped in plaid short-sleeved shirt and white cotton slacks, exited the luxury car with his driver in tow.

Both Tone and Daewoo watched Frank pluck away a half-smoked cigar, "Didn't I tell you he'd show?" Daewoo boasted. "Let's get down there. It's on." From behind the shed, Tone and Daewoo's eyes locked onto the courtyard's opening. Both had firm grips on their guns and stood ready to shoot if the wrong face appeared.

Frank rounded the bend with a quizzical look at his surroundings. Behind him, his driver, all 110 pounds of a long-beaked man with hollow eyes and an intense sneer. Both appeared out of place. Both ceased walking when the two hijackers strolled from behind the shed twenty feet from them.

"Hey, Frank," Daewoo greeted casually.

Frank advanced two paces. "You fuckin', cocksucker," he drawled. He nodded to the envelope the driver carried. "This is how you repay me for lookin' after you…bring me in this filth to extort money from me? I'll have your fuckin' balls for this."

Behind Frank, the driver nodded his endorsement as if he'd gladly accept the task.

"You took care 'a me all right!" Daewoo barked. "Sold me the fuck out!" He pointed the gun at Frank's chest. "Just give the money up and save the rap." Daewoo stepped to the podium, into the camera's view.

Frank collected the envelope from his driver and walked to the podium. He fingered the two keys Daewoo had placed on the racks. "What the hell is this? Where's the rest of the stuff?"

"Don't worry, you'll get it," Tone informed him.

Frank shot a daggered stare at Tone. "You bet your Chinese ass I will. Who the fuck is this guy anyway?" he asked bitterly.

"I'll show you who the fuck I am," Tone offered. He pointed the 9mm. at Frank.

"Hold up! Don't shoot 'em!" Daewoo screamed. He pulled Tone's arm down. "Just get Stoney and the coke for me?"

After a tensed pause and a deadly glare targeted at Frank, Tone reluctantly lowered the gun and walked off. Daewoo turned back to the mobster. "Why set me up, Frank?"

"I had nothin' to do with it."

"Don't hand me that shit. You knew the Serragucchies were gonna slump Fontes and you used me for a scapegoat."

Frank's face was tomato red and he spoke with fire. "Let me tell you somethin', you fuckin' dick. Everybody takes orders from somebody. I found out after Fontes was iced."

"And you expect me to believe that?"

Frank slammed the envelope down on the racks. "I don't give a shit what you believe. All I know is that you done dug your own grave. Here's the damn money. Now tell Bruce Lee to bring me my coke!"

On beat, Stoney entered the courtyard with Tone's gun tucked just beneath his ribcage. Stoney's hands were still tied behind his back and he dragged a small piece of rope from an ankle. He looked disheveled as the driver went about untying his wrists.

Frank, still in the camera's eye, pointed a stubby finger at Daewoo. "Your ass is mine," he said stiffly.

"Ask me if I care," Daewoo shot back, wondering if indeed the mafia's arm stretched as far as some claim.

Tone snatched the envelope and tossed a plastic bag at Frank's feet.

The driver rushed to peek in it. He flashed five fingers at Frank, who scratched behind one huge ear.

"Where's the rest?" Frank asked.

Daewoo looked to Tone, who slid a wrinkled sleeve across his nose and sniffed.

"Call it a fee for the fuckin' you gave my man," Tone answered.

"You shut the fuck up, you shithead chink!"

Frank spat. Tone's smirk became a sneer, and before Daewoo could protest, Tone had already raised the 9mm and sent a peal of vibrating thunder across the courtyard.

Traffic was sparse. The few rubbernecks that walked the morning streets, twisted their heads as Ryan pushed the Plymouth near its limit toward Washington Avenue. He weaved past a tan carrying BMW, gratified his hunch had paid off.

After interviewing Stacey Baker, Ryan decided to put a tail on the girl. He'd sensed there was more to her unprovoked attitude, her shiftiness, her evasiveness. In Stacey, he saw the classic indications of a young woman protecting a boyfriend.

He turned onto Washington Avenue and pulled alongside a dark blue sedan and leaned from the window. "What's going on?" Ryan asked the bearded detective behind the wheel.

"They count five boxed in the rear, so far. You won't believe who showed."

"Who?"

"Frank 'The Fingers' Rosso."

Ryan paused in thought before nodding. "How about backup?"

"They're spread along the perimeter. Cadowski thought it best. Already, several of Russo's men have been picked up; all carrying. We also picked up the girl leaving with two kilos tucked in her bag."

Ryan thanked the detective and found Sergeant Cadowski in a parked, unmarked van three buildings from the warehouse.

In the van, five uniformed officers were crouched around the sergeant receiving assignments.

Ryan squeezed in among them. "Tell me they're our

guys," he said.

"I can't say for sure," said Cadowski, "but it seems these guys are into some serious business."

Cadowski was all spit and polish, six-two, 240 pounds with colt-blue eyes and not a hair on his tight muscled face.

"Can we get to them?" Ryan asked.

"I got an eyeball on them. It looks like a drug deal going down. I'm open for suggestions."

Ryan took in the surrounding faces. All rookies. "Anyone here <u>not</u> wearing a vest?"

One officer raised his hand. "Get one," Ryan ordered.

Halfway through the briefing, every head spun at the sound of a gunshot.

"MOVE OUT! MOVE OUT!" Cadowski barked, leading the charge from the van with his assault rifle readied.

Everyone in the courtyard stood motionless. Only Tone stared coldly at the fallen body, sprawled among the bundles of cocaine. The others looked on unbelievingly.

A large chunk of the driver's face had been blown away, and the thin man's limbs continuously twitched.

"Now who's the chink, mob man? Keep running' your mouth and your ass'll be next," Tone warned.

"We gotta get outta here," Daewoo said quickly, rushing to the shed and snatching the tape from the camcorder.

"Get that shit and come on!" Tone called, gun targeting Frank.

Daewoo was already backpedaling toward the warehouse when Frank, unable to control his anger, yelled, "You're a dead man!"

"Then I might as well slump your bitch-ass now, huh?" Tone spat. He took better aim at Frank, poised to blow the Italian's head off. From the corner of his eye, Tone spotted the first cop turn the bend. In one swift turn, Tone reeled off two rounds that chipped the wall's edge.

The cop retaliated with two shots of his own, both short left-wingers into the ground.

Stoney watched Tone and Daewoo disappear into the warehouse and took off after them.

Behind Stoney, the officer took aim. Ryan snatched down the cop's arm.

"Christ, they're getting away!" the cop squealed.

"No, they won't. They're surrounded." Ryan pointed to Frank, who'd laid spread-eagle on the ground. "Cuff him and take him out of here."

The warehouse roof is of tarred asphalt and fenced with redbrick topped by a layer of grey cement. Broken bottles, old sneakers, and other debris littered it coarsen black carpeting.

Seven-stories the warehouse stood. And although Daewoo had reached the roof with plenty of time to descend its drainpipe, the two police cruisers below prevented him from doing so. He'd also ruled out retreating down the stairs because twenty yards from him loomed Stoney with a glare of hatred aimed in his direction.

Daewoo began explaining himself immediately. His words were more of a plea; although, he was the one carrying the gun. "I swear it wasn't me, Stoney." He pulled the videotape from his waistband and offered it. "Here. Check it out for yourself."

Stoney stood quiet. His glare unchanged.

Daewoo saw images of Grim Reapers in the man's eyes and knew his plea had fallen on deaf ears.

"Put the gun down!" Stoney barked.

"I can't do that, rodie." Daewoo stood close to the roof's edge. Every few seconds he'd peer down at the cruisers, hoping they'd rescue him. He knew he'd enough on tape to clear himself of the crimes, but, if he was to shoot Stoney, an unarmed man, he'd likely serve that life sentence he'd been avoiding nonetheless.

Stoney stepped forward. Daewoo tried pleading once more.

"Stoney, man, I'm telling' you…this tape will prove I ain't have shit to do with it."

"If you didn't, put the gun down." Stoney stepped even closer.

"Stay away from me. I ain't no killer, but don't push me."

"You're right. You ain't a killer, so put the gun down."

Daewoo was confused. Over the edge, he looked, wondering if he jumped would he break his legs. There had to be a way.

As he rifled through his confusion, his eyes never veering from Stoney easing even closer, he fired a warning shot that tore up a chunk of asphalt just to the right of Stoney's feet. His second shot was short and to the right. Then, with an unexpected, sideways launch, Stoney had slapped the gun from Daewoo's hand and, with herculean strength, slammed him to the rooftop. Stoney snatched up the gun and caught Daewoo scampering away. Stoney's first blow struck home. He landed the gun's butt flush against Daewoo's jaw and sent him crashing back to the asphalt. The second blow cut deep into his cheek. A spew of blood and teeth flew from Daewoo's nose and mouth and small whimpers escaped him only to heighten Stoney's fury. Stoney's hand was covered in blood.

As he raised the .357 to land another blow, he paused to take aim. This blow knocked Daewoo unconscious Tears of anger streamed down Stoney's blood-speckled face as he stood straddling Daewoo's lame body with ugly images of his mother's death flooding his mind. He pointed the magnum at the mask of blood Daewoo wore. For months he'd waited for this moment, the chance to revenge his mother's death and end the haunting nightmares. Never had he taken a man's life. As much as he tried pulling the trigger, images of his mother, his father, his son, Sheila, and all that was good in his life flashed behind his eyes - interfering, something he felt was unfair. He answered the images by closing his eyes and reeling off a storm of gunfire. Each pull of the trigger carried its own message.

When the thunder has ceased, Stoney opened his teary eyes and stared down at the bloody mess beneath him and felt an easiness.

"Drop it!" Cadowski screamed from the roof's doorway.

Without looking from the body beneath him, Stoney let the gun fall from his hand.

Ryan reached Stoney first and pushed him from over the body. He knelt and placed two fingers on Daewoo's throat.

"At least you had the sense not to kill him," Ryan said, taking notice of the shredded asphalt beside Daewoo's head.

Tone hit the cement stairs in a panic, tripping over the first few, gun gripped tightly. He cursed his shortsightedness for not inquiring about an escape plan. Daewoo had disappeared, and in a frenzy, Tone's eyes swept the second floor flat for a hiding place to dodge the first wave of cops. He tucked into a small utility room at the far side of the flat.

"They're headed for the roof!" a cop cried as the swarm of officers passed by the floor.

When the shuffling ceased and all seemed quiet, he crept open the door just enough to peek from its crack onto the stairwell. He held the gun high with both hands and held his breath, afraid his breathing, uneven as it was, would be heard across the spacious flat. He watched and waited till beads of nervous perspiration dripped from his face onto the dark, dingy tiles at his feet.

His body was still numb from his night of snorting. Never had he ingested so much cocaine in one night, and as his adrenalin increased, so did the cocaine's effects. His body temperature rose dramatically, and his lack of breathing forced him into a fit of shivering. His paranoia began rising to an uncontrollable height. He decided to make his move.

Tone pushed open the closet door, sprung to the stairs, and hit the first-floor landing at a full sprint.

"HOLD IT RIGHT THERE!" one of three officers shouted.

Without aiming or slowing down, Tone let off three shots in their direction, catching one of the officers in the neck. Before the stunned officers could draw their weapons,

Tone was through the open door, sprinting to the shed zigzagging low to the ground. With ten yards to go, an onslaught of gunfire exploded behind him. He dove to the truck's front tire and scurried around its opposite side. Bullets exploded around him, tearing at the shed's aluminum walls and snatching junk from the shelves as they zipped by. He ripped open the truck's door and threw himself inside. He quickly worked on the truck's wiring until its engine roared to life.

In the past, he'd stolen plenty of cars equipped with stick shifts. His experience showed when he jerked the truck into gear and tore from the shed, head barely above the steering wheel. A hail of bullets bounced off of the truck. Some embedded themselves into the truck's body while others shattered the windows, sending shards of glass raining into the coach.

As Tone rounded the hook leading to the byroad on four flat tires and speedometer nudging 60, he felt the truck bucking over two-by-fours and iron crates Daewoo had scattered about earlier. Halfway through, the iron horse stalled, and plumes of white smoke surged from its engine. Tone fought to restart the truck. Nothing happened.

Several stalks of wood had snapped the truck's two A-frames, and a well-placed bullet had crippled the engine.

Tone knew he'd reached his end; he peeped over the steering wheel at the two police cars blocking the entrance.

Both cruisers' doors were open. Four cops kneeled behind them, poised to shoot.

Behind the truck, Tone heard the yells of more officers closing in. He checked the gun's clip. It was empty.

"Shit!" he yelled. All around him, he heard screams. "GET OUT OF THE TRUCK! TOSS YOUR WEAPON OUT AND EXIT THE VEHICLE WITH YOUR HANDS UP!"

Tone thought them a joke. No way, he thought, would he allow himself to be jailed for the rest of his life - or be given the death penalty. "I'll come out alright," he mumbled, still having difficulty breathing. Deeper his breaths became as he prepared to have his court day on the streets.

Without the patience of thought, Tone kicked open the truck's door and charged the police barricade with his empty gun held high.

The first bullet struck fast, tearing a chunk of flesh from Tone's right thigh. The second and third bullets struck in succession, hitting him squarely in the chest, sending his small, wiry frame stumbling backward. Tone raised the weapon once again, this time, he attracted a barrage of gunfire that lifted him from the ground and slammed him into the front of the truck. Slowly his limp body slumped to the ground with unseeing eyes wide open.

Rays of sunlight poured through the state prison's barred windows, illuminating the millions of motes, drifting weightlessly throughout cell block F. It was cleanup time. Early morning. And like usual, Philadelphia-bred convicts gathered around the television lofted from the ceiling. The morning news was on, and the topic: the new, mini po- lice station's opening in south Philadelphia's Martin Luther King Project.

Captain Plummer, rosy-cheeked with smiles, looked on as an enthusiastic Mayor cut the ribbon on the new precinct then shook his and several other officials' hands.

But the precinct's opening was not the story that piqued the state convicts' interest. Their anticipation lied on the follow-up story surrounding the trial of Frank "The Fingers" Russo and their fellow convict, David Stokes.

The convicts watched the anchorwoman as if each of them had a stake in the trial's outcome. In a way, each of them did. It was their *"Code of Ethics"* at jeopardy: Honor Among Thieves. Secretly, each convict felt Daewoo had gotten a raw deal, had been framed mainly because of his own greed. But still, there was the code they live by regardless of the empathy felt for the ex-addict standing just a few feet from the crowd, alone, leaning on a mop stick, watching the news broadcast as well.

"Here, your dumb-ass go again, Daewoo," a huge, bald convict shouted while the others held smirks and eyed the television.

Daewoo frowned at the colored sketch of him testifying during the trial covered the screen. He could barely speak then. The braces holding his broken jaw in place, had made it near impossible for him to testify. There hadn't been much to say anyhow; the tapes had told the story.

He lowered his head and went about mopping the cellblock floor, wondering if the word he'd received about Stoney getting married and Ryan having been his best man was on the up and up.

He thought about Trina's distorted face when the judge had sentenced him to three to ten years for conspiracy to assault a police officer. The officer Tone had shot during the mayhem would pull through. Daewoo was thankful for that and the District Attorney dismissing kidnapping and drug trafficking charges in exchange for his testimony against Frank and the Serragucchies.

He finished his mopping detail and shuffled to his cell feeling miserable. Tape to the bars was a loose-leaf sheet of paper with the word "Snitch" scrawled big as day. Inside the cell, his property lies strewn in disarray. His new home had been ransacked. He swallowed to conjure the strength to do a hard fifteen-year bid. He fought back the tears and tried to handle what he knew was the start of a new fight.

THE END

www.ingramcontent.com/pod-product-compliance
Lightning Source LLC
Chambersburg PA
CBHW071512110726
47908CB00003B/807